THE BEST PEOPLE YOU KNOW

CHARLIE RHOADS

THE BEST PEOPLE YOU KNOW

Her inheritance was a writhing bag of snakes, but Delia was no snake charmer.

Delia Jameson can't catch a break. Her job sucks, her ex-boyfriend cheated on her, and now her beloved great grandaunt GeeGee died, and Delia can't even get to the funeral. Imagine her surprise when the lawyer informs her she's inherited GeeGee's entire fortune.

Immediately, her slimeball ex appears on her porch, trying to win her—and her money—back. An old friend from summers past also slides in, asking her to dinner despite not seeing her for a decade. Worse, she keeps getting disturbing texts from an unknown number.

When someone breaks into her house, she begins to fear more than the opportunistic men in her life, and when she starts reading GeeGee's diary full of troubling secrets, she's even more afraid. Will Delia survive her windfall? Or will she lose everything and everyone as she discovers her true inheritance?

Copyright © 2023 by Charlie Rhoads

Cover created by Covers by Stella

All rights reserved.

No part of this book may be reproduced in any form or by any electronic or mechanical means, including information storage and retrieval systems, without written permission from the author, except for the use of brief quotations in a book review.

❦ Created with Vellum

Dedicated to

my beloved sister Joely, always

Special thanks to:

my editor, Sherri, for all the financial knowledge

1

"Ms. Cordelia Jameson. Such a pleasure to finally meet you."

Delia took the offered hand for a businesslike two-pump shake with the elderly lawyer across the desk. "Please, just call me Delia. Everyone does."

"Of course, Miss Delia. Won't you please sit down?"

She did so, as did Edmond Langston, Esq. Or so the expensive-looking name plate on his desk said. GeeGee had been known to call him Eddie in a long-suffering tone, usually with a roll of her eyes.

Delia felt a wobbly half grin quirk her mouth. Oh, GeeGee. What did you do this time?

"Now then." Mr. Langston—who did not invite her to use his first name, let alone Eddie—pulled a file folder nearer and opened it, perusing the contents. "The rest of the family has already heard the will reading, of course, but I understand completely your struggles to get here. So hard for a working woman to make sudden travel arrangements."

Working woman. That was a joke. Delia wouldn't insult the memories of hundreds of thousands of slaves by calling her job slavery, but she did an astounding amount of work for a pitiful paycheck that barely covered her rent and utilities, let alone expenses. Worse, she worked in a cramped, dingy little office with three other harried, exhausted, cranky women, none of whom liked each other, all competing volume-wise when they had to be on the phone at the same time.

She was a Help Desk tech in the IT department of an online chatter company she couldn't bear to name in casual conversation. She didn't have the dignity of being considered a working woman. It took her entire paycheck to get to St. Louis a month after missing the funeral, and she had no idea how she'd make rent now.

But it was for GeeGee. Delia would do just about anything for GeeGee, alive or dead.

"The details are fairly straightforward," Mr. Langston continued, his vaguely Southern accent at odds with his sleek suit and tidy, iron gray goatee. "Your great grandaunt left a few small bequests to other family members, a rather large bequest to the local humane society chapter, and the rest entirely to you. There are a few formalities, forms to sign, notarize, and file with the county, but "

"I'm sorry." She couldn't have heard that correctly. "Sorry to interrupt, but did you just say...?"

Though initially annoyed by the interruption, Mr. Langston smiled indulgently at the repeated apology. "I did, Miss Delia. Our dear Miss Virginia left the bulk of her rather sizable fortune to you. That includes all her stock holdings, several land titles scattered over the country, the house and acreage outside the city in Webster Groves, and all the contents therein. It's all yours."

He handed over a report of some kind that Delia was, frankly, too flummoxed to make sense of. All she could see was the number of digits to the left of the decimal point. It couldn't be right. That wasn't a real number, was it?

Shocked to the core, Delia slumped back into the cushy, leather chair and focused on breathing. She couldn't even begin to absorb the implications of what he'd just said and shown her. GeeGee had... what?

"Are you alright, dear? Do you need a glass of water?"

She blinked several times and shook her head. She was not, in fact, all right, but she did not need a glass of water. She'd probably just choke on it.

"No, thank you. I'm just... I can't even... oh, GeeGee, what have you done?"

His steely gray eyebrows rose. "I'm sorry? Is this not good news?"

She huffed incredulously. "Of course it is. It's... but it's too much. Too big." She gave the papers in her hands a flap. "I don't know how to run a... an estate. GeeGee was a whiz at everything, but I'm just a Help Desk lady. What do I know about the kind of wealth she built?" She put a hand to her forehead. "Oh, god, she built that fortune from the ground up! What if I lose it all? Oh, GeeGee, what did you do?"

"Now, now, you don't have to worry about a thing, Miss Delia." His tone was soothing, commiserating. "Even your great grandaunt couldn't personally run an estate this size all on her own. She had accountants and lawyers and a trust management firm and all sorts of folk who helped her keep it all in order. You'll have access to all of those same people if you like. Or you can pick whoever you want. But please don't worry that you're being pitchforked into a whirlpool without at least a boat and paddle."

She huffed again, mildly relieved. It was starting to set in a little. A fortune. The grand house in the country. A *fortune*.

She shook her head and looked at Mr. Langston, actually seeing him now that the worst of her blind panic had passed. "Mr. Langston, what do I even do right now?"

He smiled benevolently. "My dear Miss Delia, you may do

whatever you want. You can go back to California, secure in the knowledge that you need never work again unless you choose to, or you can move back here and take up residence in The Hollows. Your great grandaunt loved that piece of property more than any other and built that house from her own plans, so it wouldn't be a surprise if you wanted to spend some time there to get your bearings. I understand you spent plenty of time there in your youth, so it would be a familiar place to let it all settle in."

He sorted the papers he'd ruffled, then closed the file folder and laced his fingers together over it.

"Or there are five other properties prime for development all over the country that you could choose to build your own home on. Frankly, Miss Delia, the sky's the limit, though it's usually best if you don't make any huge purchases the first year. Just until you're more used to your new lifestyle."

Again, she felt overwhelmed. Such a vast fortune didn't even compute in her head. And it was hers. All hers. Oh, GeeGee.

She suddenly felt like crying, despite the impossible windfall.

"I think I'd like to stay at GeeGee's, at least for a while." She sniffled but thankfully didn't break down into a sop of tears. "Just until I get my bearings, like you said. But… what do I do now? It can't be this easy. How long will all this take?"

Mr. Langston smiled benevolently again, relieved that she apparently wasn't about to dissolve into a watering pot after all. "I'm afraid it will take some time for all the signatures to process and the holdings to be transferred. There will be taxes, of course, on such a large inheritance."

She felt herself getting swamped again, but he saw her expression turn brittle and quickly changed directions.

"But that's not a problem for today. Right now, I'll put you in touch with the money people and get you some cash forwarded to tide you over until all the paperwork is done and all the legal mumbo jumbo is sorted out. All you need to do for today is get yourself something to eat and go on home to The Hollows. Get some rest. Veg out, as my grandson says." He looked at her with sincere understanding. "Get your head around everything that's happening, alright, Miss Delia?"

She took a deep breath and nodded. "Alright, Mr. Langston."

"And you call me if you need anything. Day or night. Here's my office line, and my personal cell number is on the back. It's always on."

She wanted to scoff at having as distinguished a lawyer as Mr. Langston's own cell phone number, but instead, she was gobsmacked all over again by the fact that she now had the kind of money that bought a lawyer's private cell number. What on earth was happening?

She walked out of the cushy office feeling like her head was floating about ten feet above her body. She didn't feel good yet. Maybe that would come with time. She didn't even feel relief that it seemed her life of Help Desk drudgery was over, and freedom beckoned. It was too soon for those feelings. She wasn't there yet.

Instead, she forced her numb fingers to order an Uber on her old phone with its cracked screen, then just stood there outside the office like an idiot, staring unseeingly at the passing traffic and trying to get her brain to absorb the impact. All that money. GeeGee's big, crazy fortune. All hers.

Did not compute.

She was so rattled, in fact, that she didn't realize the Uber had arrived until the driver rather impatiently blipped his horn at her. She startled, then hurriedly climbed in with an apology. And just like that, she was whisked off into her future.

The briefest thought surfaced, then was swamped back down again. She hoped that, for once, it was a happily ever after sort of future.

2

The Hollows was GeeGee's rather gothic name for her large home property and its deliberately witchy, Victorian-style house. It always sounded so romantic to a young Delia, like something out of one of her mother's beloved books about young maidens lured into gigantic houses by shady older men with secrets hidden in basements and attics.

Now, she stood before the house with her overnight bag strapped across her chest, a few plastic bags of rudimentary groceries heavy at her side, staring up with new eyes. Because this wasn't GeeGee's house anymore. It was Delia's.

The mental equivalent of the Blue Screen of Death threatened, so she shook off the thought and climbed the wide steps to the sprawling, wraparound porch. The old swing swayed gently in the crisp fall breeze, not moving enough for the chains to squeak but enough to grab her wandering attention. She and GeeGee spent so many rainy mornings in that porch swing, tall glasses of iced tea in hand, talking about school and boys and plans for the future. And GeeGee's latest spell work, of course, much to Delia's mother's discontent.

Delia shook off the memory and went to the third pot of

mums from the left side of the door. She shifted the pot aside and took the key underneath. She would, presumably, get GeeGee's keys when all the paperwork was settled, but for now, she didn't think GeeGee would mind her using the spare to get in. The poor woman hadn't had time to make preparations for her death. The stroke came completely out of nowhere.

Apparently, all the crystals and herbal tea in the world couldn't prevent something like that.

Tears threatened, so she grimly unlocked the door and pushed inside. The house yawned around her, the foyer dark and not as welcoming as it used to be when GeeGee was alive and usually hurrying to engulf her in a huge, patchouli-scented hug. Oh, what Delia wouldn't give for just one more of those hugs, one more chance to talk to the woman who had been so much more than a great grandaunt to her. More than just a duty visit to some distant, elderly relative.

"GeeGee."

Sighing, her breath trembling a little, she flipped on the light in the foyer and watched some of the warmth come back into the room. GeeGee's cardigans hung neatly on their wooden pegs along the wall by the door, her wide-brimmed, floppy gardening hats tucked over them in a neat row, the array of sandals and garden-grimy tennis shoes lined up against the wall underneath. Pictures of relatives both living and dead dotted the walls, smiling a welcome or watching silently with neutral expressions as this usurping child, this interloper, intruded on their solitude.

Everywhere she looked, she felt GeeGee's touch. The soothing mauve tones of the walls and the natural wood trim. The cardigans and photos. The stained-glass shade on the hanging light overhead that lent cheer to the large entryway.

Forlorn and helpless, she looked to the left at GeeGee's parlor, where the grand old dame sometimes held séances at the big, round table with its spindly, velvet-cushioned chairs or did tarot readings for those brave enough to ask for the truth. Ahead, to the dining room and the dark kitchen beyond. To the right, where the staircase climbed over the entrance to the living room and the little hall that led back to the guest bathroom and then further back to GeeGee's suite.

This wasn't Delia's house. How could it ever be? It so achingly, perfectly belonged to one Virginia Falkirk, deceased but impossible to live without.

Her cell phone rang in her jeans pocket, and she startled, then put down her grocery bags to dig it out and look at the cracked screen. Julie. Oh, thank god.

"Hey, girl." Julie's warm, understanding voice washed over her like balm. "How are you holding up?"

"Oh, Julie, I don't even know where to begin."

"Oh, honey, don't cry."

A strangled laugh choked out of her. "I'm not crying, I promise. I just... it's so much to tell that I don't know where to begin."

Julie made soothing noises. "Well, don't start at the beginning or anything lame like that. Start in Australia or Mongolia or Zaire. That's always a lot more interesting."

Somehow, she managed to laugh while her throat ached. "I am so glad you called."

A smile warmed her friend's voice. "Good. Now spill. What's going on, girlie?"

"I'm a bazillionaire."

"*What?*"

She huffed, though she pulled the phone away from her ear a little at the shrillness of Julie's voice. "I said what I said."

"Cordelia Jameson, you tell me what's happening right now!"

She closed her eyes and leaned back against the door. She hadn't even made it past the welcome mat. Jesus.

"GeeGee left me almost everything, including the house. I can't... Julie, I don't even know what to do. I've been standing here in the foyer for like half an hour trying to get my mind around it, and it just runs into a brick wall every time. What do I do?"

"Jesus Christ, Delia!"

"Right?"

Julie laughed, sounding almost hysterical. "You're rich! Like filthy, stinking rich!"

But at what cost? she wanted to ask but didn't. GeeGee knew she would never have traded her for the money.

"Not quite yet. Apparently, there's a lot of paperwork and transferring of funds, but I'm supposed to talk with the money guy tomorrow about some cash to tide me over until it's all settled."

"You have a money guy!"

She grinned, finally feeling like the expression was right on her face. "I have a money guy. Can you believe it?"

"I cannot." Some of the astonishment went out of the friendly voice. "But I'm so, so happy for you. You deserve something good to happen for you for once."

Delia didn't know about that, but she did feel better after telling her friend. "Look, it's getting late here."

"Two hours ahead, I know."

"Right. And frankly, I'm completely done in by today. Travel was a bitchkitty, but getting the news wiped me the rest of the way out. I'm gonna go upstairs, take a hot bath, and stumble into bed and sleep for twelve hours straight."

"That sounds like an effective prescription, Dr. Jameson." Julie sounded amused. "You should do that."

"I plan on it." She smiled softly. "Thanks for calling, Jules."

"You know it. Get some rest. Absorb. Call me tomorrow."

"Will do. Goodnight."

She tapped the End button and put her phone away, then picked up her grocery bags and finally stepped off the welcome mat. She stopped briefly in the kitchen to stow the groceries but avoided the hallway back to GeeGee's room. Instead, she went directly upstairs to the gable room GeeGee always kept ready for her, though Delia hadn't been able to visit more than once in the last five years, thanks to her shitty job that sucked her life away without any PTO to show for it.

She and GeeGee talked, of course, practically every week, but it had been almost three years since she'd actually laid eyes on the old girl, and even that had only been for a weekend. And now, she never would again.

"Oh, GeeGee."

It felt as if the whole house sighed around her as she wearily walked down the hall to her room. She opened the door and felt homesick, even though she was practically home. The room had every comfort GeeGee could think of for her favorite great grandniece. Hand-sewn quilt on the luscious queen-sized bed. Blackened brass light fixtures on either side of the ornate wrought iron headboard. Bright hand-hooked rugs on the hardwood floor. Shelves of books and an exquisite rolltop writing desk with a cushy leather office chair. A gaming center opposite the rolltop, complete with cutting edge computer set-up, huge TV, and two gaming consoles.

And the window seat in the gable, of course. Cushioned and strewn with colorful pillows, that seat had been the scene of many a blissful summer reading day as a young Delia spent weeks at a time with her great grandaunt while school was out.

So many memories. All that was missing was GeeGee herself.

Heartsore, Delia crossed the room with dragging steps, hauling her carry-on strap off over her head to drop it on the bed. Her ponytail got caught and pulled, and she felt tears spring to her eyes, but she angrily blinked them away and tossed the carry-on down with more force than was strictly necessary.

Just... she'd never been in the house without GeeGee in it. Even as a teenager, she'd always go with the good lady if she left to go to the garden or take a walk or run into town. She loved spending time with her favorite relative, so where GeeGee went, so did little Delia. It felt weird to be here without her.

But this was hers now, and it was so, so wrong.

Sighing as the spurt of anger sapped her remaining energy, she rummaged through the bag for a pair of underwear and a t-shirt, then dragged her feet over to the *en suite* bathroom GeeGee had insisted on when Delia started spending longer and longer stretches of time with her. She had her own clawfoot tub with a separate shower alcove, and all the décor was in soothing shades of cool green and sandy tan. She looked with listlessness at the shelves of lotions and soaps and bottles and bath bombs, all made by GeeGee herself.

Not patchouli, she told herself. I don't need to cry in the bathtub. I won't be able to open my eyes in the morning if I cry any more today.

She picked a vanilla rose scented bath bomb, turned on the hot water, and plugged the drain. The tub filled slowly, steam rising into the chilly fall air. She probably should have turned on the heat before coming upstairs, but she hadn't thought of it. Didn't matter, anyway. She could grab another quilt out of the trunk at the foot of the bed. It would smell like cedar and weigh her down deliciously.

When the water was as deep as she wanted it, she climbed in, then dropped in the bath bomb between her knees. She loved this process, the foaming, the rising of scent, the rolling of the little bomb as it got smaller and smaller until it vanished, the slow spread of the color cloud. She'd made so many bath bombs with GeeGee, spritzing the dry mixture so it would hold together without activating the baking soda, matching scents from the dozens of little brown essential oil bottles, choosing from Dead Sea salts or Epsom salts, charcoal or flower petals, glitter or no glitter.

Sniffling, she wiped at a stray tear, then dipped a washcloth in the gentle pink of the steaming-hot water and gruffly washed her face. Her eyes would be swollen tomorrow from all the tears and now from this rough treatment, but what did she care? She wouldn't be seeing anyone, anyway. This wasn't a social call.

When she was sure she'd washed away every trace of saline, she re-wet the cloth, then leaned back against the sloped tub and draped it over her face, letting the damp heat seep into her pores. She and GeeGee sometimes gave each other facials with expensive treatments from Korea. She could practically hear GeeGee explaining that the moist heat would open her pores, so she should do any serums or moisturizers quickly so her skin would soak up all the good stuff.

She didn't know if that was true. She didn't care. She wasn't in the mood for a facial tonight.

When the water cooled enough to remind her that it was chilly in the house, she sighed and sat forward, then used the washcloth to actually wash. Standing up and drying off felt like a Herculean feat, but when she was done, her skin felt silky and smelled like a freshly blooming rose with a hint of sweet vanilla, so she supposed the bath had done its job.

Finally feeling numb after a day full of painful jabs, she shuffled to the bedroom, pulled out the promised quilt, spread it over the bed, then crawled under the whole lot. She hadn't brushed her teeth, but she doubted she'd get a cavity overnight. And she didn't really care if she did. Hell, she could afford a whole new mouth if she needed it.

But that thought threatened to spool her back up, so she pushed it away and let the exhaustion win. She slumped into the cushy mattress, swallowed down a sob or two, and finally, thankfully fell asleep.

If she cried in the night, well, it hardly made a difference come the morning.

3

"I'm sorry, how much did you just say?"

The money guy—Barry? Gary? She couldn't remember now what he'd asked her to call him—cleared his throat nervously and stammered over his answer.

"Uh... a h-hundred thousand, ma'am... er... miss. Ms. Jameson."

Delia closed her eyes. She'd done as directed by Mr. Langston and called the trust management company, who had forwarded her to her own particular money guy. She had no idea what to expect, but she couldn't have even begun to expect... *that*.

"Ms. Jameson?"

"I'm sorry," she heard herself say into the phone that felt at the end of a hundred-foot-long arm. "I must have misheard you. You must have said a hundred or a thousand, right?"

More nervous throat-clearing. "Uh... no, actually. I said a hundred thousand." He sounded ridiculously nervous. Why on earth did *he* sound nervous? "Is that not enough?"

She nearly dropped the phone, her fingers numb and nerveless. She hadn't misheard. This guy was really prepared to just *give* her a hundred thousand dollars. And he didn't think that was enough.

"I could possibly arrange to have a little more in a few days, but—"

She burst out laughing. It wasn't a good belly laugh. It sounded ragged around the edges and not particularly nice, and she tried like hell to cut it off before she offended this man with his hand on the purse strings.

"I'm sorry. I'm so sorry. I just… you can't be serious." She huffed, her eyes feeling too big for her skull. "You can't really mean to just give me a hundred grand, just because."

Some of the nervousness left his voice, and she realized he must have been worried about how she would react to what he clearly thought was a low-ball number. That low-ball was more than twice her yearly salary.

"Given the full amount of your holdings, Ms. Jameson, a hundred thousand is, forgive me, penny candy." He huffed a little himself. "If I'm honest, I didn't expect your reaction to be laughter. At least, not laughter because I was forwarding you too much."

She wiped wearily at her eyes, which had watered with disturbing ease all morning when she so much as thought about her reason for being here. Which had really been watering the entire month that GeeGee had been gone.

"Please call me Delia, Barry. It was Barry, right?"

"Uh, Barrett, ma'am. Er, Delia." He cleared his throat. "Are you alright?"

She must have sounded as heartsick as she suddenly felt after her burst of laughter. She sighed.

"No, Barrett, I'm sorry, but I'm really not. This is all way too much for me. I had no idea… I mean, I never thought GeeGee… my great grandaunt would ever…."

"I understand."

You don't, she wanted to say but didn't. You couldn't. Not if you work with money like this every day. Not if you think a hundred thousand dollars is too small an amount.

"But I want you to know that I and your team are all here for you to help make this transition as easy as possible. And yes, that includes forwarding you an amount to tide you over for expenses until the rest of the estate is fully in your control."

Her heart pounded painfully in her chest. "But I don't know how to control an estate. I'm in IT, not finance."

"You don't have to worry about a thing, Miss Delia. That's what the team is for. Even your great grandaunt, formidable woman that she was, needed help keeping track of everything. We're here to help. I swear it."

She swallowed hard. "Did you ever meet her?"

Barrett's voice warmed. "Miss Virginia? I did. Not many times—we mostly conversed over the phone or through email—but on rare occasion, she would come to the city to deal with us or her CPA firm directly. She much preferred The Hollows or being off on her travels than skulking around in St. Louis, but we sometimes needed old-fashioned signatures. She would always bring us home-baked treats. A very kind woman, and brilliant, was Ms. Falkirk."

Delia nodded. "She is. Was." She swallowed hard again. "I guess.... If she trusted you and this team, I'd better do the same. I've never gone wrong following her example."

"A wise decision." It sounded like he was finally smiling. "Now, if you could just give me your banking information, I'll have this money wired to your account. You should have it by this afternoon. If you need any cash before then, I can have some couriered to you."

She blinked. "Are you kidding?"

"No, Miss Delia, I am not." He sounded amused.

"Oh. Uh, that won't be necessary. I'm not planning to go anywhere right now, and I got some groceries on the way here.

Mr. Brinkley cleaned out the fridge after the funeral, you know, because she...."

Because she hadn't known she would die like that, Delia thought. Because she didn't know it was her last day, and all the food would have rotted in the fridge if not for Mr. Brinkley's kind interference.

"Miss Delia?"

She blinked rapidly, her stupid eyes watering all over again. "Yes, I just... had a moment. I'm fine. Um, do I need to sign anything?"

"Not yet. This is just a preliminary advance. Your lawyer will have all the paperwork when it's ready for you to sign with the notary in his office. Is there anything else I can do for you at the moment?"

She tried to think. She really did. But her brain was floating ten feet above her body again. This man was wiring her twice her yearly salary for her to blow on anything she wanted, and that was a drop in the money bucket compared to what she was about to receive. Her aunt was as financially savvy as she was disdainful of capitalism and the government. Her fortune was vast, despite all her charitable contributions every year. Delia wasn't sure she even had a mental grasp on how much it was, despite the balance report Mr. Langston had shown her.

"I don't think so, Barrett. Thank you." She swallowed hard. "For being understanding."

"Of course, Miss Delia. You take care, and if you need anything, you call that number my secretary gave you. He'll put you through any time, night or day."

She felt the laugh pressing at her throat again but managed to swallow it down. Here was yet another fancy, important person who had just invited her to call night or day. Because she was an important person now that she had money.

Sighing, she put her phone down on the coffee table, scooted sideways into the cushy couch, and lay down with her head on its pillowy arm. She tried to lie on her back and stare at the ceiling, but that felt too open, so she curled up on her side, instead, and stared across the salon and its streams of glorious morning light. It was barely ten o'clock, and she was already a hundred thousand dollars richer than she'd been when she arrived.

This was GeeGee's favorite room in the house besides the kitchen. This was where she taught little Delia to read tarot cards over Mom's protests. Where they had secret séances at the round table with one of Delia's local friends when she was a teenager, which would have sent Mom through the roof if she ever found out. It was the site of many a real tea party with GeeGee's favorite Darjeeling tea and scones and little tri-corner sandwiches with the crusts cut off.

It was a beautiful room done in deep reds and roses with brass and ivory fixtures. Not real ivory, of course, because GeeGee could never stand for the slaughter of elephants, but as close to real ivory as fake could be, creamy and smooth instead of plasticky. The brass was real, though, as was the lustrous patina.

Sighing, Delia closed her eyes and wondered if she could fall back to sleep in this favorite room, then sighed and got up to go into the kitchen. It was where GeeGee spent a large portion of her time, baking and cooking, canning and preparing her own fruits and vegetables, bottling and tubbing lotions and potions and salves and, of course, bath bombs. This kitchen was her workspace for both mundane and magical workings, as she often said with a little wink.

It, too, was a beautiful room, this time done in harvest shades and rich wood, with butcher block counters, an island, two ovens, a larger than necessary fridge, and a pantry leading off to one side. A glass-windowed door led to the greenhouse that butted up against the kitchen on the outside. Just like the one in *Practical Magic,* a young Delia always said, usually before begging GeeGee to jump off the roof and fly.

She sniffled, then swiped at her nose and strode over to the fridge to rummage around for fixings for brunch. She'd awakened too late for a real breakfast, but she'd bought enough groceries to make a GeeGee specialty. English muffins, mascarpone cheese, and eggs. She'd even splurged for avocados, despite the perilous state of her bank balance. Perfect for a poached egg sandwich, just like GeeGee loved for her own breakfast or brunch.

Delia wasn't up to her great grandaunt's level of cooking, but she knew her way around a kitchen well enough, and she'd practiced this particular meal many times over the years of staying here. She'd even made it for GeeGee a few times for birthday breakfasts when she was allowed to come in the spring as well as the summer. Mom didn't care for avocados, but it just wasn't the same sandwich without them, as far as Delia was concerned.

Call her a millennial. She didn't care.

Grinning a little, she went to the little breakfast area in the window nook and sat down with one leg folded up under her. There, she looked out the windows at the lovely fall colors of the trees and the bursting mums out on the back patio while she ate her brunch and sipped a glass of the passionfruit mango juice GeeGee always kept in the pantry until it was opened and placed in the fridge. This side of the yard was still mostly in shade early in the morning, but by now, it had taken on the bright rays of midmorning and everything out there seemed to glow with ethereal light. It was lovely. Bittersweet.

GeeGee loved autumn. She adored spring for all the planting and watching things grow, and she loved summer for the flowers and the fruiting of the garden, but fall was her favorite time. It was Delia's favorite time, too. Harvest time. Mild days and even milder evenings, bonfires and pumpkins, hay bales and corn husks. Halloween, her favorite holiday, though she hadn't celebrated in years. Since she moved to California.

Was it ruined now? Would she ever have another autumn without a hint of melancholy, knowing it was without GeeGee?

No. GeeGee wouldn't want that. She'd be appalled at the very thought. Delia would just have to toughen up and find a way to move on.

Her phone chimed, and she picked it up and then cursed. What on earth—

"What."

Her tone was flat and brooked no nonsense.

"Well, nice to hear from you, too."

The voice of her ex-boyfriend rushed over her like a fever, both hot and cold, and she wanted to throw her phone. "What do you want, Luke?"

He sighed. "I heard about GeeGee. I wanted to make sure you're okay."

"How."

He paused, likely at her icy tone, and she grit her teeth together.

"On the internet. Seriously, Delia, are you okay?"

"Why do you care?"

Another pause. She crossed one arm over her ribs, her fingers gripping her phone too tightly.

"Honey, I'm just checking on you. Can't we at least be civil?"

"No. You're the one who dumped me, so you don't get me civil anymore."

Her face burned. How dare he call her after how he treated her.

"Delia—"

"I don't know what you think, but I'll even admit you were right about one thing. It's over, Luke. Don't call me again."

She punched the End button so hard she almost jabbed her finger through the cracked glass. The nerve of the man. He'd dropped her like a wet pair of pants after two years of dating, then ignored her for six months, so there was no way he'd just called to see if she was okay. If she knew Luke Sullivan, he'd been fishing. Seeing how much she might have inherited from GeeGee, who he knew was loaded. The bastard.

She looked at the rest of her brunch with loathing. She couldn't eat another bite. She'd choke if she tried. Sighing through clenched teeth, she got up, shoved her phone into her jeans pocket, and took what remained over to the trash to dump it like he'd dumped her. Then, she rinsed her plate with jerky motions and propped it in the dish drainer to dry. When she was done, she propped her hands on the edge of the sink and took deep breaths.

As if everything wasn't already terrible without a call from her smug ex-jackass calling to feel her out about a windfall. What would he do if he found out she was worth a fortune now? Surely, he would never know. She rarely talked to any of their old friends these days, since they'd all sided with him in the break-up, and while GeeGee was rich, she didn't make a spectacle of herself enough to make the papers for anything other than charitable works. Other than an obituary, which wouldn't say who got the dough, there shouldn't be any sort of announcement he could find.

She should be safe from further predation. She hoped.

Her shoulders eased down with this reasoning, and she bit her lip. She'd thought she was in love with him, but she wasn't sure anymore. It hurt like a bitch when he dumped her, when all her so-called friends started ghosting her when she called, but from a distance, she could see that he'd been all wrong for her, and so had they. They weren't really her friends, and he hadn't been the man she thought he was. He couldn't even keep a terrible steady job, let alone a good one.

But she'd spoken to GeeGee almost every night for a week, sobbing her heart out, before she finally got that particular message, and it took months for it to fully sink in.

God, she missed GeeGee. If only she were here now.

Not that Luke would have ever called her without some excuse. But still.

Sighing, Delia turned away from the sink and left the sunstruck kitchen to get on with the rest of her day. Luke was old territory. She had an entirely new future to plan, starting now.

4

Should she be doing something?

Delia wandered the house, debating if she should be... what? Packing GeeGee's things? Why? It wasn't like she could bear to get rid of them. To store them, maybe? What for? She was the only one who would likely want any of GeeGee's things, anyway. Oh, there were other great grandnieces and nephews, of course, and a few cousins who might want something, but most of her paternal line, where she was related to GeeGee, was long since dead. Including Delia's own father, though she didn't like to think about that time of her life.

So she should leave things where they were and just... what? Live upstairs in her childhood bedroom? Admittedly, it was a swanky room and just as appealing to her now as it had ever been, but she felt weird at the idea of living up there when GeeGee's whole life had been downstairs.

Should she move into GeeGee's room?

But she shied away from that thought. It wouldn't be right. She'd never sleep another night if she tried to live in there, surrounded by GeeGee's favorite possessions, the familiar, well-loved patchouli scent breathing all around her. No way.

She supposed she shouldn't do anything just yet. Not until the papers were signed. Until then, her brain insidiously whispered, anything could happen. Someone could try to overturn the will. How had the rest of the family reacted to hearing about Delia's windfall? Did anyone else have expectations?

Delia really didn't know her more distant relatives, and she knew her paternal side even less, besides GeeGee. After her father died, there just didn't seem to be any urgency to keep in touch on either side.

Were they angry? Were they threatening with torches and pitchforks? Should she give Mr. Langston a call and ask, or would that just stress her out worse?

Shaking her head, she went into the parlor, picked a deck of tarot cards from the drawer at random, and sat down in one of the spindly chairs at the round séance table to do a reading for herself. Mostly, she wanted to shuffle the cards. A mindless activity that kept her restless hands busy while her mind thought.

Shuffle, shuffle, shuffle. She really shouldn't be stressed yet. Even if, by some miracle, the will wasn't overturned or challenged, she'd have to go back to California to put in her notice and get her dingy little apartment packed up before making any hard decisions. Shuffle, shuffle, shuffle. That was only if she decided to stay in Missouri instead of living in California. But what was there for her in California, anyway? A broken heart, a bad job, and an even worse apartment?

Shuffle, shuffle, shuffle.

Ten of swords. A painful but inevitable ending. That part had already happened. Poor GeeGee was dead of a thunderclap stroke. She'd probably been dead before she hit the dirt in her beloved garden.

Nine of cups. Live it up. Enjoy life's riches and pleasures. She supposed that could be her present, as the usual three-card spread—past, present, future—suggested. She was certainly being invited to live it up, what with a fortune soon to be hers.

The Tower. Reversed.

She shivered. The Tower always denoted a time of catastrophic change, but reversed usually meant loss, obstacles, a volatile situation impossible to be avoided. The only way out is through, GeeGee would say if the Tower showed up in a reading, usually shaking her silvery white-haired head, her mouth set in sympathetic lines.

The Tower showing up in a reading for the future….

She shook her head and swept all three cards back into the deck. She didn't believe in tarot. It was all the power of suggestion, cold reading, and educated guesswork. GeeGee was astonishingly good at it, obviously, but that's all there was to it. As much as a young Delia had fully believed in GeeGee's witchcraft, grown-up Delia knew it was mostly the spicy therapy choices of an aging hippie who'd led an interesting but sometimes harrowing life of government protest and struggle in the mostly male world of business.

The wind chimes hanging over the patio from the corner of the greenhouse chimed suddenly, the sound loud in the silence of the house. She hadn't heard any particular wind blowing, but she was inside. Coincidence, Delia told herself, though her fingers felt suddenly cold.

But… she'd been thinking of GeeGee's practice of the paranormal, and those handmade wind chimes out on the patio had clamored for attention.

Ridiculous. She wasn't thinking what she was thinking. GeeGee had fully believed in ghosts, but even she never thought the house itself was haunted. Visited by the spirits she supposedly called up during her séances, but not haunted in and of itself.

And Delia didn't believe in ghosts any more than she believed in tarot readings. The wind must have been a gentle one that wasn't audible inside. Simple as that. It happened all the time, she was sure. She just hadn't been here in a while and wasn't used to the sounds of the house.

Just the same, Delia thought she was done with the tarot cards for today. They hadn't told her anything she didn't already know. The past was done. Her present was tentatively full of riches and pleasures. Her future was a dark and shadowy mess that she couldn't see clearly through all the smoke of destruction. Spicy therapy at its finest.

Her phone rang just as she was tucking the tarot deck back into the drawer with the other decks. She looked down at the screen and debated answering, then felt like the worst daughter in the world.

"Hello, Mom."

"Oh, Cordie, honey, how are you holding up? Did you get back to Missouri okay? I was so worried when I didn't hear from you last night."

It wasn't a veiled reminder that she should have called as soon as the airplane wheels hit the tarmac. Her mother was a sweet woman who was incapable of in-the-moment meanness, but it hit home, just the same. Delia had forgotten, what with all the fluster over her inheritance.

Jesus, did Mom even know?

"I'm okay, Mom. Holding in, anyway. Have you talked with the lawyer yet?"

"Lawyer? No, why would I? I have nothing to do with that side of the family."

She wanted to laugh, but her throat was too tight. "She left it all to me, Mom."

"I'm sorry?"

She closed her eyes. "GeeGee left me almost everything. The house, the property, everything but a few bequests. Mom, she gave it all to me."

"Oh, Cordie, I don't know if I should laugh or cry!"

The tears decided for Delia and started to flow between her tight-shut eyelids. "Oh, Mom, I miss her so much—"

"Cordie, honey...."

Wiping her eyes, Delia shambled over to the cushy couch and sank down onto it, curled up on her side with her phone pressed to her ear, sobbing like she had when she first heard the news. GeeGee had been a cornerstone of her life, and now, she was gone. It felt like Delia's foundation was shifting, and not in a good way, despite the money. And the property. And the house.

"I know you miss her, honey." Mom's voice sounded soothing, calming, like when Delia was young and had a fever. "But she knew how very much you loved her, and she clearly wanted you to be happy if she left you everything."

"I know," Delia sobbed. "But that just makes it worse. It feels like... like... like profiting off her death."

"No, sweetheart, that isn't it at all."

But that's how it felt. It was some of the wrench she'd been feeling ever since the lawyer spoke those crazy words that had changed everything. Maybe it was why she couldn't figure out what she was supposed to be doing here with GeeGee gone. She felt like an impostor, like a thief.

"You and GeeGee had so many good times together. She knew you loved spending all your free time with her."

"But I hadn't been here in years."

"Not out of choice, honey. And you called her all the time. You knew she was gone before I did. You were the first person Mr. Brinkley called because everyone knew you loved her so, so much."

Mr. Brinkley was the neighbor who did the heavy landscaping when it became too much for GeeGee to handle on her own. Tree branches down, groundswell disrupting her flagstone paths, the koi pond's fountain leaking, or the big pond overgrown with algae. Even the mowing, once GeeGee was too frail to push her ancient push lawn mower anymore.

He'd found her in her kitchen garden, dead with her eyes open in the row between the beets and the cauliflower. A snail had oozed up onto her cheek, leaving a silvery trail of slime. He'd told her that in a horrified whisper before stopping himself and apologizing. Delia couldn't get the image out of her mind. Or how much it would tickle GeeGee to know how she'd traumatized her landscaper.

"She wanted you to be happy, Cordie." Mom's tone warmed even more. "You deserve to be happy."

But the Tower is coming, she wanted to say but didn't. Delia didn't suppose death would change Mom's mind on the subject of tarot divination being both wicked and, perhaps worse, tacky.

"Are you at the house?"

Delia nodded, sniffled, and made herself vocalize. "Yeah. It's... it's rough, Mom. I feel her everywhere, but she's not here. I've never been here alone."

"Do you want me to come? I can hop in the car and be there in four hours. Just say the word."

She sighed. "No. Don't do that. I know you hate driving at night."

"It's not night, sweetheart."

"But it will be by the time you get here. I don't want you getting into an accident. Hitting a deer or getting creamed by a semi. I can't lose anyone else."

Another sob threatened, but she throttled it down ruthlessly. No more crying. Well, no more sobbing, anyway. She couldn't always help her eyes from watering, but she didn't have to make a damn show of it.

"Okay, okay." Mom murmured soothingly. "It's gonna be alright, Cordie. You know that, don't you?"

She supposed that was true. GeeGee did seem to have

wanted to make her life easier, anyway. Things were complicated right now, but Delia suspected she was the one complicating things herself, and the dreaded Tower she felt looming over her was all in her mind.

"Yeah," she finally said, all in a rush of released breath. "Yeah, I guess so."

"That's my girl. You take it easy up there, and if you need anything, even just to cry on my shoulder long distance, you call, okay?"

"Okay, Mom. Thanks."

"I love you, Cordie."

"Love you, too."

The phone went dead in her ear, so she let it fall the inch or so to the couch cushion and sniffled, rubbing at her nose with her sleeve pulled down over her hand. Her eyes felt all hot and bleary, her throat hurt, and she sensed a headache coming on. She hated crying. She never got any sense of catharsis from it. It just made her feel more miserable.

"What do I do, GeeGee?" she whispered. "Oh, spirits, please come through to us. Spirits, speak."

But this wasn't a séance, and she wasn't surrounded by gullible yokels about to piss themselves as someone knocked twice for yes and once for no. GeeGee never resorted to such parlor tricks, but someone always did it for her. Someone inevitably couldn't wait for an answer from the spirits and knocked for themselves. It was the same as college kids using a Ouija board in a darkened dorm room. Someone always moved the planchette.

Sighing, Delia closed her eyes and debated trying for a nap. Her eyes throbbed, hot and achy, and her nose needed a good blow and some moisturizer. And she really wanted a glass of cool water for her aching throat.

No. No nap. Maybe she should suit up and go out into the garden instead. It's what GeeGee would have done.

Oh, GeeGee. What do I do now?

But the spirits weren't in a talkative mood, so Delia wearily pushed up from the couch and headed for GeeGee's collection of gardening hats just inside the door. The garden beckoned, and she must heed its call.

It was her garden now, after all.

5

Her phone chimed as she bent over the last half-row of cabbages, and she almost dropped it in the freshly turned dirt as she tried to answer it with dirty gardening gloves on.

"Sorry! Hello? Hello?" she asked as soon as she pulled off one glove and picked up her phone.

"Miss Delia?"

She pulled the phone away from her face to check the number, and yes, that was Mr. Langston, the lawyer, from his office phone. She hoped nothing was wrong.

"Yes, Mr. Langston?"

"How are you this afternoon? Are you holding up?"

She blinked, surprised at the seemingly sincere question. "Uh, yeah, I think so. Doing a little of GeeGee's gardening." Her lips trembled. "There were already weeds everywhere, and so much produce has gone to waste since… since she's been gone."

"Weeds are bad like that." He seemed to know it wasn't the weeds or the rotted vegetables that had her voice quavering. "Well, I hope I haven't caught you at a bad time. I just wanted to tell you that some of the paperwork should be all ready for you to sign by Friday, if you'd be so kind as to come into my office so my notary can earn his paycheck."

Her eyebrows shot up, her moment's wavering gone. "Friday? Is that even possible?"

His tone warmed, sounding amused. "It is when you have a competent law firm and very good estate planning at your back. Plus, I gather you made a good impression on Mr. Davidson. He was quite willing to put things through in a hurry. Your great grandaunt chose her team wisely."

Davidson, Davidson... she drew a blank. "I'm sorry... Mr. Davidson is...?"

"Your trust manager, Barrett Davidson."

"Oh! Right, right." Had she even heard the man's last name on the phone? She couldn't remember. She'd been too boggled by a hundred thousand dollars being considered penny candy. "Sorry, it's been a crazy couple of days."

"I'm sure it has."

"Anyway, I don't know if I can get to California and back by Friday, Mr. Langston. Is there any way we can push it off until Monday?"

A moment's quiet fell into the conversation like a stone in the middle of a still pond. She could already feel the ripples, though she didn't understand them.

"You're planning to return to California, then, Miss Delia?" His tone was careful, reserved. "I thought you would want to stay at The Hollows."

She blinked. Why did he care?

"Er, I guess I've mostly decided to stay here, but I'll have to go back to quit my job and pack up my apartment. That sort of thing."

His tone evened out. "Oh, I understand, but surely you realize you don't have to do any of that yourself. You never need to work again if you don't want to, and you could always hire a firm to pack your apartment and ship it right to your door." His tone warmed into amusement again. "In fact, you don't have to do anything you don't want to ever again, I dare say."

She stared unseeingly at the glory around her, gobsmacked and unable to catch up. She'd never considered not doing things herself or not putting in notice. She'd never considered that she could just… like… have someone do stuff for her. She'd always done things for herself.

Money really did move mountains, though she supposed her dinky little one-bedroom apartment counted as more than an anthill.

"Miss Delia?"

She got a hold of herself. "Sorry. I just… that never even occurred to me, but I guess you're right. I really could just hire someone to pack it up and ship it to me. And what has that job ever done for me, huh? I didn't get to come see GeeGee for the last years of her life because of that job. I missed her funeral!"

She was suddenly furious and tempted to throw down the trowel in anger. She didn't, but only because she didn't want to accidentally behead a cabbage.

"That's the spirit." He sounded genuinely pleased by her show of irritation. "Google yourself a good moving firm, send your boss an email, and cut ties completely. I'd much rather have you here at home where you can always stop by if you need us than so far away."

But her fit of pique wasn't quite done yet because she couldn't help but assume he just wanted to make sure he kept her business now that she was an heiress. He wouldn't want to lose such an enormous account.

Uncharitable, her mother's voice in the back of her head whispered. She smirked a little in response.

"Well, I hadn't really decided on anything long term, Mr. Langston, but I don't see any reason to dilly dally if I can get things done long-distance. I guess I can meet you on Friday, after all. What time is good?"

"Whatever time works for you, Miss Delia. Are you a morning person, or would you prefer the afternoon?"

She considered. "I guess I'm a morning person when I have to work, but now, I think I'll take a crash course on sleeping in. How about just after lunch?"

"Wonderful. Consider it scheduled."

"Thank you, Mr. Langston."

"No, Miss Delia, thank you. I'm so glad you're staying. Miss Virginia spoke of you so often that I know she'd want you to be quite at home at The Hollows. She'd love to know you're staying."

A wave of sadness rolled through her, but she didn't cry. She just nodded, then murmured a goodbye and hung up. She stuffed her phone back into her pocket, pulled her glove back on, and went back to work.

She'd only finished the row of cabbages and was just about ready for the dreaded beets/cauliflower convergence where GeeGee died when her phone chimed again. Sighing, she took off one glove first this time, then pulled out the phone. She immediately wished she hadn't. It was Luke again.

Cursing, she jabbed the Ignore button, shoved her phone back into her pocket, and pulled her glove back on. Her phone almost immediately went off again, and she said her absolute favorite curse as she pulled her phone back out to give the man a cussing he'd never forget.

But it wasn't Luke this time.

"Julie?"

"Delia," her friend said, sounding glad that she'd answered. "How's it going down there in the wilds of the back of beyond?"

She found her first real grin of the day and propped her free hand on her hip. "You'll be happy to know that some of the paperwork to make me a bazillionaire will be ready by Friday. Unless lightning strikes, you're talking to a very rich lady who… well, sorry, Jules…."

"Sorry? Why? What's wrong?"

It only now occurred to her that not coming back to California probably wouldn't be a good thing for Julie. But it wasn't like Delia couldn't still visit. And surely Julie would want to come see the home place now that it was hers?

"Er... I guess... I'm not coming back to California."

"...Oh."

"Yeah."

She rushed on, hoping to explain and soften the blow. "I just... the lawyer said I didn't have to worry about ever working again, so I didn't really need to put in notice, and I can hire a firm to pack up my apartment and just ship it to me, and...." Desperate, she went on in a somewhat pleading tone. "But you'll come see me, right? And I can always do with a trip to California."

She trailed off, feeling like she'd just kicked a puppy.

"You know what?" Julie sounded surprisingly positive. "Good for you. That job sucks, and so does your apartment. You don't need that hassle."

Her eyebrows shot up for a second time on the day.

"I'm glad for you, Delia. And you're right—I can always come for a visit, and so can you. What's half the country between friends like us?"

Relieved beyond belief, Delia felt her breath whoosh out of her on a somewhat hysterical laugh. "Exactly! Especially with me paying for everything, and don't even argue about it."

"Wasn't going to." Julie sounded smug. "A rich lady like you won't even notice the cost of a round trip plane ticket."

She propped the phone between her ear and her shoulder to take off her other glove. "Honestly, I didn't really think about staying here until the lawyer brought it up. I knew I'd have to be here for a while to settle everything up, but... well, I haven't been thinking long term, what with everything being sprung on me like that. Everything's happened so fast."

Julie made a sympathetic sound. "I get that."

"And then, it just seemed like staying was the obvious choice. I mean, I guess I could go anywhere I wanted, but there's really only one place I've ever wanted to be besides California, and other than you, California really didn't work out for me."

"Oh, honey."

"I know, I know." She took the phone back in hand. "Oh, did I tell you that Luke called?"

"What? Why?"

"He wanted to, I dunno. Commiserate with me over GeeGee's death, I guess. I hung up on him."

"Good for you. That snake." Julie sounded like she wanted to punch a pillow. "How on earth did he even know?"

"He said he saw something on the internet. More likely, a formerly mutual friend saw something on the internet and told him, and he thought he'd see how much I was worth and how likely I was to take him back now that I'm worth something."

"Pssh. You were always worth a lot more than that dirtbag."

"That's an insult to dirtbags everywhere, Jules."

She snickered. "True. Good on you for hanging up on him."

"After him dumping me one week, then showing up at all our favorite places with a new bimbo on his arm the next? And all our friends taking his side? Yeah, he's lucky I didn't reach through the phone and strangle him."

"I still say that's the better option."

Delia snorted. "If I could have, believe me."

They were quiet for a moment, then Delia sighed.

"Look, Jules, I'd love to talk, but I'm standing in the middle of GeeGee's garden, trying to keep the weeds from getting a foothold now that this place is my responsibility. Talk to you later?"

"You know it." Julie sounded like her breezy self again. "Although you could probably hire about ten gardeners to do it for you."

Snorting, she shook her head. "I'm hanging up now."

"Just sayin'. Hot, shirtless gardeners."

"Goodbye, pervert."

She hung up, shoved her phone in her pocket, and pulled her gloves back on. She couldn't help but wait a moment, though, just in case her phone rang again.

Then, when she was sure she was alone for good, she took her chosen weapon in hand and went back to her weeding and soil-turning.

The day rolled on around her.

6

The money hit around seven o'clock in the evening. Delia wasn't haunting her bank account. She really wasn't. But she *had* checked it at least a dozen times over the course of the day, and she'd just about convinced herself it was all a big joke on her when... boom. Her balance ballooned to $100,034.72.

She stared at the number on her phone's cracked screen, her eyes so wide they hurt a little. She had a hundred thousand dollars. How many months had she stressed over whether to eat ramen and pay her rent or risk being late to get in the odd salad? How many times had she passed on buying new business casual wear because she couldn't pay her electric bill *and* have a new shirt without any stains or holes in the armpits? How many times had she walked in the heat instead of riding the bus because she didn't have bus money?

Her knees buckled and she sat down hard on the floor in the kitchen because she wasn't near a chair. The vegetable medley in the wooden steamer on the stove sent up fragrant moisture, the water underneath bubbling merrily. The beautiful old German clock ticked serenely. The breeze blew outside, jingling

GeeGee's wind chimes at the corner of the greenhouse just outside the window nook.

She had a hundred thousand dollars. It might as well be a million. What would she even do with all that money?

And it was an *advance*. Not even a drop in the bucket.

She looked down at her battered old Wal-Mart sneakers, her faded jeans washed thin, her t-shirt that did actually have a hole in the armpit. She could buy herself a pair of Docs. Designer jeans. A thousand flannel shirts.

Would she? She didn't think she even had the imagination to use the sort of money coming to her. Hell, she couldn't imagine how to use a measly hundred grand.

The timer on the stove went off, and she swiped out of her account, shoved her phone into her jeans pocket, and clambered to her feet. She washed her hands, then dealt with the steamer basket. She wasn't a vegetarian, by any means, but she always ate more vegetables at GeeGee's than on her own because GeeGee had vegetables coming out of her ass, thanks to her abundant garden. At home in California, Delia couldn't afford vegetables. She could only afford shelf stable foods. Anything that went bad too fast was too expensive to replace.

She could have grilled a steak out on the patio, as well. GeeGee had plenty of beef both in the freezer and in the deep freezer in the pantry. She'd just butchered a cow she bought from a neighbor who raised them organically. They were all Delia's steaks and roasts and pounds of hamburger now. She might as well make the best of it, but she'd forgotten to lay anything out to thaw until she was already hungry.

So, for tonight, she steamed broccoli, cauliflower, and carrots, and sauteed okra and zucchini in butter with fresh-grated parmesan scattered over the top. She added a block of tofu with soy sauce because she needed some protein with all the vegetables, or she'd wake up starving in the middle of the night. Also, she was too skinny these days, but between her budget and all the stress of the past six months, she just didn't have much appetite.

It was ironic because she'd always been overweight until now. Who knew all it took was misery to lose that baby fat she'd been packing around for twenty-eight years?

Shaking her head at her line of thought, she heaped vegetables and tofu on her plate and vowed to gain that weight back. If she was honest, she'd rather be a little overweight than a lot under. She felt so fragile these days, like a gust of wind would blow her over. Frankly, she was glad GeeGee hadn't seen her, or the poor woman would have been beside herself trying to fatten her back up.

No reason not to eat now, though.

So, of course, the second she got situated at the window nook table, her phone rang. Luke again. Jesus, why wouldn't he give up? Was the siren song of money really that loud?

She supposed she'd have to block him. She really should have done so before now, but she never expected him to call her. He'd been in such a hurry to get rid of her, after all. Why would he want to talk to her?

Now that he was making a pest of himself, she ought to do the deed and be done with him. She started to swipe to bring down the hammer when she saw that he'd left a message. She stared at the notification for a long time, then grimly put aside her phone and ate her food. She didn't need to hear that message. She didn't want to hear anything he had to say.

She managed to eat most of her plate and drink down a glass of iced tea before that resolve folded on her and she listened to the message she should have just deleted unheard.

"Dammit, Delia, I wish you'd answered. I'm worried about you. I know you must be really struggling right now. I just want to talk. I want to be there for you. I know I wasn't there for you like you needed me before, but I want to be that now. Call me back, okay? I'm really worried. Bye."

She snorted and deleted the message, then immediately wished she hadn't. She berated herself because deleting it was the right thing to do, and she didn't need his empty platitudes any more than she needed him to "be there" for her. She was a grown-ass woman, dammit, and she did not need her jackass ex-boyfriend encroaching on her freedom now that she was financially free as well as relationship free.

Besides, where had he been this whole last month she'd been struggling? He must have only now remembered that GeeGee had the big bucks.

The wind chimes tinkled in a soft breeze outside, and she wished she could watch them dance, but it was too dark out there. It got dark early in The Hollows, even in summer when twilight seemed to linger forever in the meadows. The trees, of course, and the hills rising all around, leaving plenty of low-lying areas like the one the house was situated in and named after.

But this was fall, and the sun sank behind the hills by 5:30 this time of year. By the time winter rolled around, it would be drawing down dark by 4:00. She would be here then, she supposed. Would she feel less like a guest waiting for the hostess to come home? It felt like she was still waiting for GeeGee to walk through the door, as if she was just out in the garden or had run into town.

Brightening determinedly, she pushed up from the table to take her dishes to the sink to rinse. She reminded herself that she should run into town tomorrow and buy herself some new clothes to tide her over until her tiny wardrobe arrived from California. Then again, she might just burn her whole collection of shabby, worn-out business casual and buy a whole new wardrobe. She could certainly afford it, even if she never got another penny.

With a plan in mind, she put the dishes in the dishwasher, propped the steamer basket in the dish drainer to dry overnight, and tidied up after herself before going upstairs to her room. She wanted to have a nice, long bath, then maybe read for a while. A lovely, quiet evening that would hopefully lead to a deep, dreamless sleep before she went into town tomorrow. And she would sleep in. She didn't have to get up early anymore if she didn't want to.

To hell with Luke and his empty promises, she told herself as she climbed the stairs. I don't need him. I have money.

Grinning with a hint of an edge to the expression, she stripped out of her ratty old clothes, pulled on the colorful kimono robe GeeGee bought her on one of her trips to Japan, and went into the bathroom to run a full tub of hot water. She wanted a jasmine bath bomb tonight. And maybe some soft, meditative music on her phone. And candles. GeeGee had a whole shelf full of scented candles for her, along with one of those long-necked lighters.

When she was situated with her hair bundled up on top of her head and jasmine-scented hot water up to her neck, a few little white flowers floating on the surface, Delia let herself actively think about Luke's message and was relieved to realize she didn't care that she'd deleted it. Not anymore. That had been a knee-jerk response, she supposed. A little ingrained piece of her that still thought he could love her even though she wasn't sure he'd ever loved her in the first place. That was all.

Once she'd distracted herself from that instinctive response, the message had no more power over her. She let it go. And she would block him when she got out of the tub, but that was an action for Later Delia. Right Now Delia was relaxing in a tub of luxuriously scented, steamy water with a dozen candles flickering away in the dim room.

Smiling, she closed her eyes. Things were, for perhaps the first time in the past five years, looking up.

7

Delia was too excited to sleep in. Once she woke up enough to remember today was for shopping—a task she usually hated because she never had the money to make it anything but depressing—she practically threw off the covers in anticipation. Sure, Webster Groves wouldn't have the big shops that St. Louis would have, but Delia would be daunted by shopping in that big a city, anyway. Webster Groves would do just fine for this initial foray into spending without having to mentally round up the tax to ensure she didn't go over budget and have her card decline.

Unfortunately, she'd only brought the one pair of jeans—her other pair had a hole in the knee and was faded almost white by long usage—and a few long-sleeved t-shirts, plus the one flannel shirt she'd owned since college. Her options were limited. She chose the faded charcoal gray shirt because it looked like the most intentional choice under the plaid flannel, and it was supposed to be chilly out today. She stood for a moment looking at her popped-elastic, washed-out old bra, then decided to get really crazy and buy a new bra today, too.

Did she even know her bra size now that she'd lost so much

weight? She hadn't considered getting another one in the past six months, but now, the sky was the limit. Hell, she might get downright decadent and buy underwear, too. And socks.

Grinning at her ridiculousness, she pulled on her old duds, then brushed out her hair. She looked at the frizz for a moment, then impulsively French-braided it. She rarely took the time, as her hair, despite being curly, was too fine to stay in a French braid all day, but she wanted to look like she was trying. GeeGee always had a bunch of hair stuff in the bathroom for her. She'd make use of some hairspray and a couple of clips to tame the fly-aways and call it good.

She looked at herself for a long moment after her hair was up. She looked... worn out. Sure, she was dealing with fresh grief, so she had puffy, dark-ringed eyes and sallow skin, but there were lines in her face that hadn't been there before. Part of it was losing weight due to stress and upset, but part of it was also just the stress and upset. It had carved itself into her face, and she was suddenly mad about it.

Grumbling, she reached for the assortment of GeeGee-approved skin care products on the vanity and started slathering. Cold cream. Cotton pads to wipe it off. Warm washcloth. Toner. Moisturizer. That's all she really knew how to do. The rest of the array of potions and unguents were a mystery to her.

But she looked a little more refreshed, perhaps due to the scrubbing, so she called it a good morning's work and went downstairs to make herself some breakfast. She didn't get fancy. She just used a biscuit cutter to cut circles out of two slices of bread, buttered the pan, put in the bread, then cracked eggs in the holes to fry. She gave them a single flip because she didn't like sunny side up, then put the leftover circles in another pat of butter to toast.

When those were done, she took her plate over to the window nook and sat down to watch the garden while she ate. The yolks were still runny enough to need mopping up with the toast circles, so she'd done it right. Just like Mom used to make when she was a kid. Just like GeeGee used to make.

She smiled softly and dabbled the last bite of bread through the dregs of egg yolk and butter on the plate. GeeGee loved breakfast. She'd loved cooking anything, of course, but if she could eat breakfast for every meal, she'd have done it. *Had* done it at least twice when Delia was visiting.

"Eggs are like potatoes," GeeGee had said while poaching a few for Eggs Benedict one fine evening. "They seem so simple and limited, but they're good for an endless variety of things. And some things you just can't make without them."

Sighing, her smile fleeting, Delia stood away from the table, took her plate and fork to the sink to rinse, then put them in the dishwasher. GeeGee had hated the dishwasher, but she hated washing dishes even more.

"One thing I hate about having always lived alone," GeeGee had said, shaking her head, her long, silvery white hair fluttering about her wizened, elfin face. "When I cook, I'm the only one here to do the damn dishes. I didn't burn my bra to wash my own dishes for the rest of my life."

So she put in a dishwasher when she designed the house, but she never stopped complaining about it. Especially when she had to replace it.

"Oh, GeeGee."

A gentle breeze tinkled the wind chimes outside. Delia wished with all her heart that it was GeeGee telling her everything would be okay.

"Okay, old lady. Okay." She sniffled, but her eyes weren't full-on watering. Not yet. "Let's go spend some money."

But first, she had to call for an Uber. She'd have to do something about transportation if she planned to stay. GeeGee hated to drive, so she'd always called the same firm to send over a driver when she needed to go somewhere. She claimed it was to save her the hassle of long-term parking at the airport when she went on her travels, but Delia knew it was because she grew more and more scared of her failing senses and reflexes as the years passed. Back when Delia was in single digits, GeeGee drove an old red farm truck around just fine, but she'd sold it a good fifteen years ago now.

Jesus. Delia paused on the porch, one foot on the first step down as the Uber car pulled around the last twist in the long driveway. She could buy a car. A new one, if she wanted. She could do it today. Wouldn't even have to use credit, though she'd have to call her bank to clear it because she didn't have any checks.

Feeling a wash of numbness roll through her, she steadied herself with a hand on the wooden railing, then slowly made her way down the rest of the steps. She could just buy a car. Any old time. And that was with the money she had today.

Which was penny candy. How much did GeeGee actually have? Delia had been too boggled to make sense of the actual number. She'd seen all those digits and whited out.

Shaking her head to clear it, she hurried over to the waiting car and climbed into the back, then asked the driver if she could take her along the main drag to see what shops were available. The driver, who introduced herself as Patricia, seemed amenable, so they headed off toward Webster Groves' downtown.

"I've never been this way before," Patricia said, dodging an obvious pothole that Delia really should fix in the driveway. "This place has a name, right? Something kinda creepy?"

Delia grinned. "The Hollows."

"Yeah, that's it. The kids say the old lady is a witch." She glanced back in the rear-view mirror. "Sorry. Was. That was awful of me. Sorry."

But Delia's grin only slipped a little. "That's okay. She *was* a witch."

One ginger eyebrow rose. "Really? Are you?"

She shrugged. "I dabble, but I don't believe."

Patricia looked amused. "You know what they say in *Practical Magic*. You can't practice witchcraft while you look down your nose at it."

Delia chuckled. "Fair enough. And if you're gonna quote a movie, that's a good one to live by."

"Damn straight."

They rode in silence for a moment as the edge of town grew nearer.

"So… you knew her?"

Delia nodded. "She was my great grandaunt. I used to spend summers here all the time."

"Nice." Patricia nodded. "I never really saw her around much, but the few times I did, I liked her style."

"Aging hippie," Delia said with another little grin. "Soft, loose fabrics. Pants and tunics. Long, flowy skirts and dresses. Lots of costume jewelry. That was GeeGee."

"You going for the same look? You said you wanted to shop."

"Oh, I'm just getting some necessities. I guess I'm moving here and need some things to tide me over until my own stuff arrives."

"No *Pretty Woman* moment for you, huh?"

Amused, Delia chuckled. "No. Just some socks and underwear and maybe a new pair of jeans."

"Shame. I think you'd rock the hippie witch look. Is your hair long?"

"Uh… I don't… I guess it's past my shoulders. Does that count?"

"Eh, it'll grow."

Another chuckle escaped her, and she looked out the window as they neared the shopping district. "I guess I can wear whatever I want here in the sticks. Someone's gotta take over the old witch lady mantle. Might as well be me."

"Who else will make love potions for all the sad local teenage girls?"

Delia's eyebrows rose. "Did GeeGee do that?"

Bright green eyes met hers in the rear-view mirror. "That's the rumor. But they also say she held séances in her living room, so there ya go."

"In the parlor, actually."

"I really like that old lady."

Delia grinned. "Yeah, me, too."

Patricia pulled into the parking lot of a mall and slowed down so Delia could peer up at the store names.

"I don't know what I'm looking for. Where's a good place just to get regular people clothes?"

"Are you talking Wal-Mart regular people or GAP regular people?"

"Never mind. Why don't you just let me off at the food court, and I'll find my own way."

"Can do."

They drove around to the main entrance, and Patricia stopped right at the curb.

"I don't have another ride lined up, so feel free to give me a call when you're done if you need a ride back. I have lots of trunk space if you decide to go full *Pretty Woman*."

Delia grinned. "I'll do that. Thanks, Patricia."

"Didn't catch your name."

"Oh, sorry. It's Delia." She reached over the back of the seat for an awkward handshake. "Nice to meet you, Patricia."

"You, too, Delia. Have fun."

"I'll try."

She climbed out of the car, then waved awkwardly as Patricia drove away. Then, feeling some of the old dread sink back in, she turned and looked up at the mall's name hanging overhead. Shopping. She didn't even know where to start.

Sighing grimly, she set her shoulders and marched inside the mall.

8

Girding her loins, Delia walked right through the food court to get at the shops beyond. After a single glance, she kept right on walking. She didn't need bath supplies. She didn't need Bible stuff. She didn't need candles or jewelry. She definitely didn't need any teeny-bopper hip clothes.

She finally found a shop that looked more her speed and veered inside, dodging a lady with two kids in one of those front and back buggies, about a dozen shopping bags stacked up her straining arms. Poor woman. Delia had no intention of ever having kids, but that didn't mean she didn't have any sympathy for some poor lady with two that close in age.

She picked up a basket, squared her shoulders again, and looked around the store to get an idea of the layout. Like formulating a battle plan, she decided. Straight through to the underclothes first, then off toward the ladies' department for shirts and jeans. Around the outside to the checkout lines, and out the door. She could do this.

She used to need the women's department for pants and shirts, but she guessed she'd be a size sixteen or even a fourteen now. Depression and angst made for one hell of a crash diet. Probably not very healthy, though.

Shaking off the thought, she threaded through the customers toward the first section she wanted to hit. Bras were stupidly expensive. Worse, she wasn't sure what her new size was and had to try them on until she found one that fit right. Her cup size had gone down, too.

When she finally tweaked the fit until it felt just right, she picked out two in the same size and style but got one white and one nude. She wanted to chafe over the price of two new bras, but she could afford it now, she reminded herself. And she clearly needed new bras. It was fine. Everything was fine.

A pack of plain underwear followed the bras into her basket. A four-pack of ankle socks in white and gray. She debated, then added a four-pack of black socks, too. Then, she was ready for jeans.

Here was a bewildering array of styles to choose from, and she would, again, have to try things on. She didn't know what size went with what style. Did she still need the full-figure shape in a smaller size, or should she go for a straight leg? She knew she didn't want skinny jeans or jeggings. Maybe a pair of jean capris? No, it was practically winter.

Harried, she picked a seemingly simple pair of mid-rise jeans, so they wouldn't come up to her rib cage, and took them to the changing room again. She hated the changing room. It was like exercising in a hotbox. She inevitably came out red-faced and sweating, usually about to cry because nothing fit.

Thankfully, the jeans fit fine this time, so she grabbed another pair in the lighter color and headed for the shirts. She didn't need too much. Just a few to tide her over. She was no one's Julia Roberts and didn't need to buy out the damn store.

As she was flipping through the flimsy excuse for women's flannel, she thought she heard someone say her name. Her head twitched, but she knew she had to be mistaken. Surely, no one knew her here in some random store where she'd never shopped before.

"Cordelia Jameson? Is that you?"

She frowned, then turned to look at the man who had spoken her full name. Surely, she should recognize anyone who knew her in Webster Groves, but this medium-height, medium brown-haired, medium brown-eyed man was a stranger to her.

"I'm sorry?"

"It is you." He broke into a large grin that ate up his face, a dimple settling into his cheek. "I take it you don't remember me."

But she suddenly did. The dimple did it.

"Elijah?" She sounded astonished to her own ears. "Good grief, Elijah Campbell!"

He started forward as if to hug her, but she quickly stuck out her free hand to ward him off. Elijah Campbell had been her best summer friend growing up, but she hadn't seen him since… good grief, ten years ago? More?

Thankfully, he didn't seem to mind taking her hand for a solid shake. He had a good grip without being overbearing and trying to break her hand like some men did.

"As I live and breathe, Delia. I should've known you'd be in town with the death and all, but I never thought to see you here at the mall with all the normals."

She grinned a little. "Well, it's not GeeGee's sort of place, I'll agree, but all I needed was some easy clothes to tide me over for a little while."

"Oh, you're sticking around, then?"

She wasn't sure she wanted to discuss this with him. She hadn't even recognized him until he smiled. Did she even know him anymore?

Did he still prefer mint chocolate chip ice cream to the infinitely better butter brickle?

"Uh, I think so, yeah. Things are still really up in the air, but—"

She cut herself off. Did everyone know about the will? About her inheritance? Maybe it wasn't the best idea to just blurt it out everywhere. Elijah was her friend as a child, but this man was an acquaintance at best.

"I get it. A death always brings up so many changes. It's hard to see where you'll eventually come down."

She nodded, relieved that he didn't press for more information. She shifted the basket to hang over her arm so she could cross them, feeling self-conscious as she realized he was all business in slacks and a button-up shirt with the sleeves rolled up to the elbows, a tie hanging loose around his neck with the top buttons undone. Had he just come from some sort of business meeting, or was this how he dressed now?

A flash of raggedy cutoff jeans sticking to his bony legs as he jumped into GeeGee's grody old pond shot through her mind, and she grinned, unable to help herself. He grinned in response, looking a little more like his old self.

"Delia Jameson." He shook his head. "Feels like I haven't seen you in a dog's years. What have you been up to?"

She cleared her throat. "Oh, I... uh... moved to California a few years ago."

His eyebrows rose. "Wow. What do you do there?"

"I work IT for a big chat company." She managed a crooked little grin. "No points for guessing which one."

He whistled low. "I should've guessed. You always were into computers and gaming and such. I should've known you'd grow up into a genius."

She blushed, thinking of her shitty cubicle with its bad fluorescent lighting, cramped confines, and drab colors. All the stupid IT help tickets that used none of her computer knowledge and set her teeth on edge with such obvious answers that an idiot should have been able to figure out the problem.

He probably thought she was a programmer instead of a Help Desk jockey. Jesus, she needed to get out of this conversation.

"Well," she said, back to being self-conscious, "you said it. Not me."

He grinned. "I did, and I meant it. But you'll be around town for a few days, anyway?"

She nodded, shifting the basket from one arm to the other. It wasn't exactly heavy, but two pairs of jeans and all those socks weren't feather-light, either.

"At least, yeah."

"Staying at The Hollows?"

Her mouth twitched in a sad little grin. "Where else?"

He nodded sympathetically. "Well, maybe we could get something to eat some evening? I'm off work by five most nights. I'd love to catch up."

She blinked. Was she being asked on a date, or was this just gallantry from an old friend? Jesus, she was so not ready for a date. She'd only blocked her ex last night, for God's sake.

"Or not," he hurried to say, putting his hands up. "No pressure. Not asking forever after."

"Oh, no, that's not—"

He chuckled, looking absurdly relieved. "It's okay, really. I just… it's really good to see you, Delia."

She looked at him, trying to see the boy she used to know. She decided he really was there, like a ghostly underlay of the urbane businessman who stood before her. So she nodded.

"It was good to see you, too, Elijah. We'll see about getting together sometime. I just don't know how everything's gonna be with…." She gestured vaguely.

He nodded eagerly. "I totally understand. Here." He handed her an honest to God business card. "Call anytime. That second number is my cell."

She looked down at the card, astonished. He was an accountant. A successful one, if his name in the firm's title was any indication. When did he decide he liked money that much?

"Okay," she said, feeling stupid. "Thanks, Elijah. I guess I'll see you around."

"Yeah. See you around."

He gave her one last, long look and a dimpled grin, then turned and walked away with his hands in his pockets. That looked more like the Elijah she knew. One who wasn't worried about ruining the line of his slacks.

She huffed and looked down at the card in her hand. A CPA. She could hardly believe it. He'd been terrible at math.

No, she corrected herself, not bad at it. Bored by it.

Shaking her head, she turned back to the pitiful, flimsy flannel and decided she'd have to hit the men's section for a good quality, warm stock. Elijah Campbell wouldn't wear flannel, she thought. Not this new version, anyway.

Pushing aside the thought, she headed for the long-sleeved tees and left the flimsy lady flannel—and thoughts of a certain brown-eyed boy she'd known a lifetime ago—behind.

9

Delia was proud of herself as she stood on the mall's stoop with her packages. She hadn't bought out the whole store. She'd purchased a week's worth of clothing that could be washed and worn again repeatedly until her old stuff arrived and she had a better idea of what she was working with. Better still, she hadn't broken down in tears thinking about GeeGee once. She'd even managed to replace her cracked-screen phone, though not with the most recent model. She still had some scruples.

Patricia's little blue car pulled up to the curb, and the little red-headed driver hopped out to help her load things into the trunk.

"I'm so disappointed. I thought for sure you'd have at least one fancy gown in a garment bag."

Delia grinned. "No such luck. I'm a few years past prom."

"Did you at least buy yourself a fluffy, see-through dressing gown to run down the halls of that big ol' house during the night?"

That earned a laugh, the first real laugh of this awful trip. "No, I did not. I'm a little disappointed in myself that I didn't think of it. I read all the right books, after all." They slammed the trunk shut and went around opposite sides of the car to get in. "It really isn't that big a house, you know."

"Coulda fooled me," Patricia said agreeably as she put it in drive and pulled into the slow parade of traffic moving past the main entrance. "Where to now? Back to the haunted mansion, or did you have other stuff to get?"

She'd need more groceries soon, as she'd only picked up absolute necessities, but she didn't need any more clothes or shoes. She didn't want to get groceries in someone else's car. What else was there?

An idea struck her. "Hey, Patricia, what car would you get if you could have any vehicle in the world?"

Green eyes flicked to hers in the rear-view mirror. "Cooper. Bottle green. Racing stripes. Why?"

Delia sighed and looked out the window at the passing traffic. "I dunno. I'm gonna be here for a while, so I'm thinking I might have to get a car. Didn't need one with all the public transportation available in California, but it's hard to get around without one here."

"California, huh? What on earth are you moving back here for?"

She shot the driver a wry grin in the rear view. "I'm sure California is great if you have money or free time, but I had neither. No, I think I'll stick around here for a while. Get my bearings. See what I really want to do with myself."

"What, are you rich or something?" Green eyes widened. "Wow, did that old lady leave you a fortune?"

Delia sighed. "Something like that." She really shouldn't be telling people about her inheritance. "Let's just say I'm in a better place than I was. I have some wiggle room now."

"Nice." Patricia nodded. "Well, if price wasn't an object, I'd definitely get a Cooper, but if you're looking for something more cost effective, I don't know what to tell you. Don't get one of these. This one is awful on gas."

Delia raised one eyebrow. "What kind is this one? I don't know cars."

"Eh, it's really not that bad compared to an SUV or a truck. I'm just cranky because gas prices are stupid."

Which must suck when you drive for a living, Delia thought but didn't say. She simply nodded as if she understood, instead, and a little quiet fell. Probably for the best.

Elijah Campbell. His medium-handsome face popped into her mind, and she looked out the window, hoping for a distraction. She'd never thought of him as boyfriend material, not when he'd been just a good summer friend for so long, but he *had* sort of asked her on a date. Hadn't he? Or was he just being polite?

Jesus. She was so not ready for a date she didn't even know if she'd been asked on.

"Did you wanna look at cars?" Patricia asked suddenly, gesturing toward a passing car lot.

"Oh, no, not today for sure." She shuddered at the thought. "I just want to get home and... I don't even know. Read or something."

"Peopled out?"

She huffed. "You could say that."

She was mostly just still flustered over bumping into her childhood friend in the lady's section of some mall shop. Her summer childhood friend, really. They hadn't been pen pals or anything during the rest of the year. They just hung out when she was at GeeGee's. Probably why it had been so easy to lose track of him as she grew up until one day, she didn't even think of him anymore.

Her phone buzzed, and she took it out, then immediately scowled.

"Whoa, that's not a good look. I pity the fool at the other end of that line."

Delia tried to rein in her scowl, but she couldn't help herself. Her caller was Luke's other phone, which she found when he'd already been texting the other bimbo while still dating her. She wasn't snooping. She'd just seen the second phone and wondered whose it was. The yet-unread texts on the lock screen had left little doubt.

She didn't remember when she found out the other number, but it was etched into her brain along with Luke's main phone. She hadn't even considered blocking the sexting phone, as Julie called it. If she'd thought of it at all, she wouldn't have thought he'd have the balls to call her on it.

She declined the call, then blocked the number. Jesus, what a day.

"Feel better?"

She looked up and caught Patricia's green eyes in the rearview mirror.

"Much."

"Good."

They drove on, leaving the town and all its wonders behind them.

10

The bad thing about new jeans, Delia learned, was that they were hard. Not tight, thankfully. Just not overwashed to the point of feeling like loose cotton. The corner point where the button joined poked into her belly button and soon wore a little sore spot. The backs of the knees folded irritatingly when her knees bent. They were stiff.

But they looked good in the mirror and fit exactly right, for all that they were uncompromising. She liked them enough to put up with the momentary annoyance. A few wears, and they'd be just right, she was sure.

She spent most of the afternoon sprawled on the chaise in GeeGee's parlor, reading a book and nibbling on veggies dipped in bleu cheese dressing. The fresh produce felt almost as decadent as a five-course, five-star meal as she crunched her way through homegrown carrots, celery, cucumbers, sugar snap peas, and the last of the cherry tomatoes.

GeeGee would be canning this last bountiful harvest, but Delia was daunted by the process—especially the potentially explosive pressure cooker—and never learned. She'd watched any number of times and always helped by chopping and washing the vegetables to be par-boiled, but the canning process itself had always escaped her. She supposed she'd have to learn now. It would be a shame to waste all of GeeGee's good garden produce just because she couldn't eat it fast enough.

But that was a problem for another day. Right now, her job was to wait for her new lawyer to call and tell her the papers were ready to sign, and, apparently, to mentally fret about what would happen if someone challenged the will. She wasn't quite brave enough to call Mr. Langston and ask about it, so she gnawed at her lower lip every time she thought about it instead.

It wouldn't matter, really. The hundred grand she already had made an enormous difference in her lifestyle. She could afford now to get a better apartment and maybe live like a person again instead of a scared little mouse in a hole in the wall. She'd even once had an idea about developing her own online cooperative game, but she'd given up due to lack of time and money. And, frankly, because Luke told her she should stick to her day job and leave the idea development to him.

Unfortunately, now that the possibility of living at The Hollows and taking over GeeGee's little empire was out there, Delia felt a stab of panic at the idea of losing it. The Hollows was home in a way her own mother's house had never been. The Hollows was a safe place away from home, the place she knew she could always go if she needed to get away or was in trouble or needed a shoulder to cry on. GeeGee had always been there, and now that she wasn't, Delia couldn't bear the thought of losing that last, tenuous connection to her safe place.

Maybe it was down to her relationship exploding in her face just six months ago. Maybe it was hating her job and her apartment and her life. The why didn't matter. What mattered was keeping The Hollows, which meant taking the money and using it wisely to keep everything going like it was before.

If that meant learning how to use a pressure cooker, well, Delia supposed YouTube had a video tutorial for that.

Her phone chimed, and she picked it up to see an unfamiliar number. She hesitated to answer, thinking that Luke might have found a new number to torment her with, but it could also be the lawyer or the money guy. Though their names should come up on her screen... unless they were calling from their cell phones. Sighing, she tapped to answer and braced herself.

"Hello?"

"Miss Delia?" It was Mr. Langston, much to her relief. He must be calling from his cell phone. She hadn't saved his number in her contacts yet. "I wonder if I could have a moment of your time."

"Of course, Mr. Langston. What can I do for you?"

"Hopefully, it's what I can do for you. As there were no objections to the will as read or to the ruling on the death certificate, and as I had a few weeks of lead time due to your not being able to make it home until now, I was able to push through some of the paperwork already. The property paperwork is ready to sign as soon as you are. I could run it over after three if that would be good for you. That way, I can get it filed with the county before end of business."

Her eyes widened. So many questions answered, just like that. "Today? Wow. I don't... I mean, of course. Although I hate to think of you coming all the way out here. I can call for an Uber and be there in less than an hour."

"Not a problem at all, Miss Delia. I know it's not the full set of keys to the kingdom, and I could hold onto this paperwork until it's all done, if that would be easier for you, but—"

"But there's no sense waiting if there's no objection?" she guessed, sitting up out of the chaise with a burst of excitement. "Mr. Langston, I think this is the best news I've gotten all month."

"Bless your heart," he said in a tone that actually meant "bless your heart", rather than a big "screw you". "I know it's been tough on you. You just let me take care of everything the way your great grandaunt wanted it, and everything will work out just fine."

Relief sagged her shoulders. "Thank you, Mr. Langston. If you really don't mind the drive, I'll be here all day."

"I'll see you after three then with my notary, Miss Delia. Until then."

"Yes. Thank you."

She tapped the End button and looked down at her phone with amazement. This was really happening. Piecemeal, but still happening. The Hollows would be officially hers by this evening. She could hardly believe it.

"I promise I'll take care of it, GeeGee."

The wind chimes tinkled gently out on the patio, and Delia looked up and around the parlor with a hopeful expression.

"Is that you? Of all the people who might turn into a ghost, I thought you, at least, would be more direct than clanking your own wind chimes."

Silence answered her, but she grinned softly anyway. Maybe she shouldn't have treated GeeGee's séances like entertainment. Maybe there really was something to this ghost stuff.

Her grin widened. Probably not. But it was nice to think GeeGee might still be hanging around, trying to help her make good decisions when it came to the fortune the woman had earned through both hard work and cunning.

Her phone rang again. This time, it was Julie, so Delia answered quickly.

"Hey, Jules."

"Hey, girl. You sound better. I take it you're adapting to the multiple body blows you've taken this week?"

She huffed. "I dunno about that, but I feel a little more sure-footed than I did yesterday. I got some clothes to tide me over until my stuff gets here, and I found out that the lawyer already has the paperwork on the house and property ready to sign. He's bringing it over this afternoon."

"Your lawyer makes house calls?" Julie sounded surprised. "Is that a country thing or a rich person thing?"

"Ha." Delia rolled her eyes. "I'm not rich yet. The money is still tied up other than the amount they forwarded me. But I'm glad about the property. I was just worrying about it maybe going to someone else and me having nowhere else to go but back to my crummy apartment and shitty job."

"It sounds like you've pretty well decided to stay there in Missouri."

She slumped back against the chaise's arm. "Yeah, I have. If this is all really happening, if it's not all some massive prank about to go horribly wrong, I feel like I belong here, taking care of GeeGee's legacy. Or whatever you call it."

"I think that's sweet. I know you loved her so much, Delia." Julie's voice warmed. "There's no one better than you to take care of what she grew."

Smiling a little, Delia crossed one arm over her ribs. "I wish we could've flown out just once so you could've met her. She was such a badass. A bra burner and a hippie and a stone-cold killer in business, all wrapped up in flowy linen pants suits with crystals in her pockets. She backed green tech start-ups that no one else would touch, and they'd flourish like her garden. Did I tell you she got arrested once for an anti-war sit-in at the capitol in D.C.?"

"Oh, my gosh," Julie said, sounding genuinely surprised. "Your great grandaunt had a record?"

"Yup. And she crocheted so many pink pussy hats that she had to ship 'em in a trunk. She backed just about anything green or women-owned and made a fortune doing it. Then, she'd turn around and donate money hand over fist to charities, and not just for the tax break."

"Wow. I do wish I could've met her. She sounds like a firecracker."

"She was." For the first time all day, Delia felt misty around the eyes. "God, I miss her, Julie. What will I do without her?"

"Burn bras in her memory, honey."

"But I just bought two new ones."

"Burn the old one, then," Julie said without missing a beat. "You talked all the time about bonfires in GeeGee's backyard. Why not build one and have your own little memorial bra burning in her honor?"

Delia considered, nodding slowly. "You know, that's a great idea. I think I'll do that." She smiled. "I think GeeGee would get a kick out of it."

"Good."

They were quiet for a moment.

"Oh," Delia said, sitting back up straight. "I forgot to tell you. Luke tried to call from his sexting phone. I had to block it, too."

"Ugh, that snake!" Julie sounded venomous herself. "I know he can't take a hint, but he ought to be able to take it stated right out."

"You'd think." She shook her head. "I just hope no one tells him there's actually money involved. If he's this persistent at the promise of money, imagine how he'd be if he ever knew I'm now an heiress."

Julie shuddered theatrically. "He won't get it from me."

"I know. And I don't talk to any of our old friends, so they won't get it from me to tell him, either. There's always the internet, but I'm hoping that this being a quaint little town in Missouri will shield me somewhat. No one cares what happens in Missouri."

Julie snickered. "That's true enough. Look, I gotta go. I'm just on my break. But I wanted to check in. Make sure you're doing okay."

"I'm fine, Jules." She shrugged. "As fine as I can be, anyway."

"Good. You call me if you need to."

"Will do. Bye, Jules."

"Bye, Delia."

She tapped the End button and shoved her phone into her stiff new jeans pocket, then sat back and looked at her book. Should she pick it up again, or should she get up and pace restlessly until Mr. Langston arrived with the paperwork?

Definitely pacing. She had too much nervous energy to read right now. Besides, she needed to tidy up from her little rabbit festival of flavors.

Grinning, she picked up her plate and headed for the kitchen to put everything away for another grazing session tomorrow. She had nervous pacing to do.

11

"That's it, Miss Delia." Mr. Langston sat back and began stacking papers together to put back in their file folder. "You are now the official owner of all sixty-seven acres of The Hollows and the house we sit in. Congratulations. Here, my dear, are your keys."

Delia looked down with wonder at her own little pile of papers and the set of keys on a plain keyring that proclaimed the house and property were hers now. It was real. It was official. The notary had made his mark.

She wanted to cry, but she couldn't do that right now. Instead, she sniffed and sat up straighter, squaring her shoulders like GeeGee taught her when she was still in single digits.

"Thank you, Mr. Langston. I so appreciate you coming all the way out here this afternoon. And you, too, Mr. Tate."

The notary nodded courteously from where he was fiddling with his stamper but didn't speak. He'd said perhaps ten words to her the whole time, and those were mostly just telling her where to sign. She didn't think he was rude, per se. Just a man of few words.

"Are you all right, Miss Delia?"

She looked at Mr. Langston. He sounded concerned, and she realized she must have let some of her need to cry out on her face after all.

"Yes, thank you. I just... I can't believe it was that easy. Just a few signatures on a few papers, and... it's not GeeGee's anymore."

He reached out and patted her hand, avuncular and warm. "I understand. We're all reeling, but I know how much she meant to you, most of all."

She nodded and looked up, trying not to be obvious about it. She'd heard once that you could stop tears from forming that way. She had no idea if it was true or not, but she was desperate.

"Anyway, I can't give you any guarantees on when the rest of the trust paperwork will be ready, but if you find yourself needing money for anything, call Mr. Davidson. I'm sure he'll be able to wrangle you another advance."

She huffed, still feeling fragile around the edges. "I can't imagine needing more than what I already have, but I'll keep that in mind. I don't know how much things like taxes and insurance on this place are. Maintenance. Any of that."

"Ah," Mr. Langston said, holding up a finger. "That reminds me. For most maintenance things, you can just call your neighbor, as Miss Virginia did, but for anything major, your great grandaunt used this contractor." He handed her a business card. "If you decide you want to add onto the house or build any new outbuildings, whatever, she knows the plans for the house and would be my first choice if I were in your shoes."

Delia looked down at the card with a watery smile. Of course GeeGee would have a woman contractor. She probably went out of her way to find one in this neck of the woods.

The name on the card was A. Wells, General Contractor, written in a simple black font on plain white card stock. She wondered what the A stood for. She supposed she'd find out at some point, though she couldn't imagine what she'd need to call a contractor about. Plumbing issues, maybe? Something wrong with the heater? Were those things Mr. Brinkley could fix, or were they above his pay grade?

So many things she didn't know. She'd never owned a house before. She'd only ever rented.

"As for insurance and taxes and the like, your CPA firm in St. Louis has things like that well in hand. If you want to look over the numbers, your lead CPA, Ms. Jenkins, would be happy to show you, but if you're simply worried about what to do, please don't be, Miss Delia. Miss Virginia had no patience for such things herself, so she wanted nothing to do with it other than supplying the money to pay for it."

She huffed again. That was so GeeGee. She was a big government protester who wanted tax money to go for social programs instead of lobbyist pockets, but god forbid she should have to fill out her own yearly taxes. And it didn't surprise her at all that her CPA was a woman. Now that she thought of it, she was surprised that her whole team wasn't women.

But that was a thought for another day.

"That's more like it," Mr. Langston said, sounding relieved. "I know it's all overwhelming right now, Miss Delia, but I promise you that your great grandaunt never wanted you to be worried about what she left for you. She made sure everything ran smoothly with only a minimum of input needed from the head honcho."

Delia took a deep breath and let it out slowly through pursed lips. "Okay. Thank you, Mr. Langston. I can't tell you how helpful you've been."

"That's what I'm here for." He stacked all his paperwork together, tucked it all neatly in a file folder, then tucked the folder into his slim, expensive-looking briefcase. "I'll get these on file with the country. I'll also call you in a few days to see how you're settling in and to keep you updated on the trust transfer process."

"How long do you think it'll be?"

He shrugged. "That's hard to say. Some cases can take eight or so months to process, but Miss Virginia was very diligent about keeping her will up to date and witnessed and keeping all her financial ducks in a row. Also, no one indicated any intention of filing any opposition to the distribution. It'll take a few months, I'd say, but hopefully not more than that."

She nodded slowly. She hadn't realized it would take that long, but she shouldn't be surprised. GeeGee had a fortune, after all, and money like that had to be carefully documented. She assumed, anyway.

"Again, if you need money in the meantime, please don't hesitate to ask Mr. Davidson. That's what he's there for."

She grinned a little, though it was crooked. "Okay, I promise."

"Good." He stood up with his briefcase, and Mr. Tate picked up his slightly larger briefcase off the floor, as he'd already been standing. "Now, I'm off, but call if you need anything or have any questions. I'll speak to you soon, Miss Delia."

He held out a hand, and she took it for a good shake, but he only held her hand gently in his.

"It's going to be alright."

She melted a little. "Thank you, Mr. Langston."

He nodded, gave a single gentle shake, then let go of her hand and turned for the door. Mr. Tate followed him out into the foyer, then out the door. She shut it behind them, then leaned her forehead against the cool wood. She was overwhelmed. All of this was really happening.

GeeGee wasn't coming back.

A few tears escaped, and she didn't begrudge them. They

were warranted. She'd just taken GeeGee's house from her legally. She knew that wasn't what had happened. She was... a caretaker. An heiress. Not a thief.

But she'd rather have GeeGee back any day.

Sighing shakily, she pushed away from the door and wiped her eyes with the cuffs of her new long-sleeve tee. She'd washed all the new clothes earlier, so the smell of GeeGee's homemade laundry soap filled her otherwise stuffy nose. It was both comforting and sad, all wrapped up together.

"You know GeeGee's recipe, stupid." She sniffled resolutely and squared her shoulders. "It doesn't have to be nostalgic when you can just make more and smell it all the time."

The sound of her own voice comforted her, and she took out her phone to call... her mother? Julie? She wasn't sure who. She just needed another voice right now.

As she debated between the two, she realized she'd missed a text from an unknown number.

> DD, unblock me. I just want to help. I still love you, no matter what happened. Let me help you get through this.

HER JAW CLENCHED. DAMN LUKE ALL THE WAY TO HELL AND back. What the hell did he think he was doing? How had he come up with yet another phone number? Did he have another sexting phone that she hadn't known about, or was it some Google group phone number shit?

Grumbling under her breath, especially at the gall of him calling her DD when he knew she hated it because it reminded her of a bra size instead of a term of endearment, she jabbed at the screen until this new number was blocked, too, then shoved her phone into her jeans pocket without making a call. If he texted her while she was talking to either her mom or her friend, she wouldn't be able to hide her reaction, and she really didn't need them going all hero complex on her. Her mother would want her to call the police.

Julie would want to castrate him with a cheese grater.

Delia grinned a little at the imagery, then headed back into the parlor to pick up her copies of the all-important paperwork and put them away. GeeGee had a little office upstairs with a filing cabinet in the corner. Delia had never rummaged around in there, but it seemed like now was likely as good a time as any. If nothing else, it might help her better understand the fortune she was inheriting.

Papers in hand, she trudged up the stairs and down the hallway opposite the one her bedroom lay down. The door to the office was open, as it had always been. GeeGee wasn't much for locked doors unless she left on one of her vacations. The office looked much as it always had—corner desk with a smart-looking laptop and printer combo on top, a few file folders in a vertical file organizer, the cushy leather office chair, and the filing cabinet in the opposite corner.

She went to the filing cabinet and tried the top drawer, a little surprised when it opened easily. If anything would be locked, it would surely be the filing cabinet. Maybe GeeGee didn't keep any important papers in there. Maybe she kept them at the lawyer's office or a lockbox at the bank or something. Delia had no idea how rich people dealt with super-secret, super-important information about themselves.

Grinning at herself, the tears past for the moment, she flipped through the neatly labeled file folders standing up in the drawer. It looked like household receipts, manuals for the appliances, and a few invoices and statements for maintenance on the same. Not pertinent to putting away her important ownership papers but possibly important for household upkeep later.

The next drawer down had a bewildering amount of stock information that she had no context for or, if she was honest, interest in. If her future depended on her understanding the stock market, she was doomed already. It was all way over her head.

Shutting that drawer, she sighed, then bent to open the third one down. This looked more likely. She wasn't sure what she was seeing, but she thought she might be looking at land descriptions of some of the properties GeeGee owned around the country. The neat little labels on each folder had names of towns and states, and the first folder she looked at contained color pictures of different sections of land, computer-drawn outlines of the property boundaries, and a packet of boilerplate legalese that she assumed equated to a legal description of the property owned.

However, none of the folders said The Hollows or even Webster Groves, Missouri, so she closed that drawer and opened the bottom one, frowning a little when this drawer only contained one file folder. It wasn't for The Hollows. It just said DELIA in GeeGee's neat capitals on the label tab. She pulled it out of the drawer and stood up, her hands suddenly unsteady.

Inside the folder was a handwritten letter, the tidy writing taking up most of the page. Delia closed her eyes for a moment, feeling tears prickling at the backs of her eyes, then took a deep breath and started to read.

Dearest Delia,

I don't know when you'll get this letter, but my sources tell me it will be soon. I know this will all be so overwhelming for you, my dear girl, but I want you to know that I know you can handle it. You are worth so much more than you've ever given yourself credit for.

Honey, there were so many times this past five years that I wanted to help you, wanted to send you money, wanted to buy you a better place to live, wanted to tell you to come back home and live with me. But I knew you had to do things your own way until you made up your own mind on what to do, and now, you'll have the funds to do whatever you want.

Make your own drawer in the filing cabinet. Fill it up with a life well-lived. I won't hold you to staying at The Hollows. I know you love the place, so you won't sell it, but I won't make it part of my will that you have to live here or anything.

This is your new life, Delia. Make of it what you will and please, please, my dear girl... be happy.

I love you like my own daughter. Always have.

GeeGee

DELIA WIPED AT THE TEARS FLOWING FREELY DOWN HER FACE WITH the cuff of her long-sleeved tee. *My sources,* she thought with a sharp prick of pain in her heart. GeeGee's spirits and tarot cards and pendulums and scrying in mirrored cups of water. Delia didn't believe in any of them, but she knew GeeGee did. Had they told her she was dying soon? Was that possible?

She laughed harshly and placed the letter back in its folder, then sniffled as another wave of tears swamped her. GeeGee never had children of her own. She was too busy living a good and busy life, traveling to far off places, marching in protests, sponsoring children in war-torn or poverty-stricken countries, crocheting afghans for the homeless, gardening.

The idea that GeeGee had loved her like the child she never had....

Working through watery eyes, she put the lone folder back in the bottom drawer, then went over to the cushy leather office chair and sat down to cry in earnest. Delia loved her mother, of course, but she'd always thought she and GeeGee had something special. A tie more meaningful because it didn't depend on duty or obligation. To see that spelled out as baldly as GeeGee had written it hurt her heart.

But it felt pretty damn great, too. Cleansing, somehow. As if the discomfort she felt at the thought of all that money could ease now that she knew how much GeeGee wanted her to enjoy it. Wanted her to make it her own.

Could she do that? She didn't know, but she thought she'd damn well better try.

Chuckling wearily and sniffling, she swiped at her face some more, then gave up and went down the hallway and around the corner to her bedroom, then on into her bathroom. She ran cool water onto a soft washcloth and pressed it over her puffy face, sighing at the beautiful sensation. The chill felt like a benediction on her heated eyes and skin.

As the moisture warmed, she rinsed it cool again and placed the cloth back over her face, cooling down even further. One more time, and she finally felt like herself again. She could practically hear GeeGee reminding her that she needed to drink some water and moisturize after a crying fit, or she'd end up dehydrated and breaking out at the same time, which would just be miserable.

"Okay, GeeGee. I remember."

Hearing her voice out loud soothed her further, so she wrung out the cloth and hung it over the faucet to dry, then reached for the fat tub of heavy-duty moisturizing cream that was supposed to be for overnight use. Delia figured she'd need it after the salt bath she'd just given her poor, ragged face, though, so she scooped up a liberal amount and daubed it on. A little massage, and her face looked dewy and smooth and not nearly as blotchy as she expected.

She looked at herself in the mirror for a long moment, then nodded once and turned to leave the room. She needed to go downstairs and drink some water.

It's what GeeGee would advise, and she'd never gone wrong following GeeGee's advice. She didn't intend to start now.

12

Delia lay on the parlor sofa again, curled up on her side with a book in front of her face, when the doorbell rang. She sat up with a jerk, then pulled out her phone to see if someone had said they were dropping by. No messages.

Eyes narrow, she scooted off the couch and stuffed her phone back into her pocket, hesitating. This was the country, after all. Sometimes people just dropped by without calling ahead. Or maybe it was her mother, having guessed how much all of this was taking out of her daughter and driven through the day to spend the night with her.

With that thought, she smiled a little and hurried toward the door.

"Coming!"

She reached out to flick on the porch light, turned the knob, and threw open the door with a welcoming smile on her face, only to feel it fall right to the floor.

"Hey, hon. Have you been crying? Of course you've been crying. Stupid question."

Luke. Luke stood on her porch. Why was Luke standing on her porch? How?

"I know, I shouldn't have come, but I've been so worried about you, DD." He stepped closer, and she immediately stepped back. He sighed. "Okay. Okay, that's fair."

She couldn't speak. Her tongue was stuck to the roof of her mouth. How was Luke here? He'd never been here before. How could he have found it all the way from California? And so fast? And why?

"Look, Delia, you need someone to lean on right now. I know things went bad between us, but can't we at least be friends? Lean on me, hon. Let me be here for you."

Her tongue came unstuck and immediately sharpened to a knife's keen edge.

"There's no money yet. You're wasting your time."

He looked hurt. "Wow. That is so not what this is about."

A laugh choked out of her. "You're here for me to lean on? Does your bimbo know? Or are you trying to cheat on her with me like you cheated on me with her?"

"That's not fair—"

"Get out of here, Luke. If you come back, I will call the cops."

She tried to shut the door, but he jerked forward, spooky-quick, and braced a hand on it to stop its momentum.

"Hey. We can be adults about this. I'm trying to help you."

"I already told you—there's no money. You're wasting your time. Go home to your bimbo." She pushed on the door, but he held it open. "And let go of my door."

She winced internally at the slip. The last thing she wanted was him knowing GeeGee had left her something, anything. He apparently would never leave her alone if he thought there was a buck to be made.

"Delia, please, be reasonable. Just because you dumped me doesn't mean we can't—"

"I'm sorry? I dumped you?" Incredulous, she stared. *"You dumped me,* and brutally, might I add, after cheating on me for months. So no, we can't be adults about this. Leave now, or I'm calling the police." When he still refused to remove his hand from the door, she grumbled. "How the hell did you find this place, anyway?"

He rolled his eyes. "Don't change the subject. I just asked the driver to take me to The Hollows. You talked about this place all the time. I knew you'd be here. And how on earth could you think I dumped you? I love you, DD. I would never—"

"Don't." Her tone brooked no argument and cut through his bullshit like an ax. "Don't you gaslight me. You cheated on me, you dumped me, and you're leaving right now. You have ten seconds to get off my porch." She pulled her phone from her pocket. "One. Two. Three."

"Look, I'm staying in town. When you change your mind about needing some emotional support, I'll be here. You know my number." He finally removed his hand from the door. "Call me, Delia. Let me be here for you. You shouldn't be alone right now."

"Six. Seven. Eight."

He sighed heavily but put his hands up and backed away. Luke Sullivan. She couldn't believe the audacity. And to claim she'd dumped him! The balls on him!

Her heart clenched as he ambled in the dark to climb back into the cab he hadn't sent away. He must have known she wouldn't be happy to see him, or he would've made sure he didn't have a way to make a quick escape. But he'd come anyway, the bastard, and because Fate was a scheming bitch, he still looked damn good in his jeans and black leather jacket, his black hair hanging in his blue eyes that always held a ghost of a smile.

A smirk, she reminded herself, squaring her shoulders. He wasn't the type of man to have a genuine, soft smile. He just had varying levels of smugness, depending on his needs at the time.

A gentle breeze blew, sending the chimes around back on the patio to jingling. Suddenly, she wanted to cry. She wished

GeeGee was here so she could fling herself into her great grandaunt's arms and sob out all the heartache she'd been bottling up for the past six months.

But GeeGee was still gone, and that was a whole other level of heartache.

Delia shut the door, then leaned her forehead against it for a moment. If only it had been Mom at the door. She could really use a hug right now.

But not from Luke. Never from Luke.

Food. She should eat something. It had been hours, after all, while she read her book.

Sighing, she went to the kitchen and turned on the light, wondering if she was falling back into the habit of eating her feelings. She supposed it was better than not eating at all, which she'd done plenty of these past months. GeeGee would want her to eat. So would her mother. So would Julie.

So, she rummaged around in the fridge for salad fixings, deciding to boil a couple of eggs and make herself a nice chef salad with tofu instead of meat. The scant groceries still held firm, but she'd need to hit a grocery store for a real haul soon.

When she was satisfied with her selections and had filled up one of GeeGee's big wheatgrass salad bowls, she went to the window nook and sat at the little round table. With the light on inside and the dark night outside, she couldn't see anything but her own reflection, but that was okay. She looked a little hollow-eyed, but that could just be a trick of the light.

Luke. On her porch. And she'd only signed the paperwork a few hours ago. If nothing else, the man moved fast.

Shaking her head, she forked in another bite of salad and chewed angrily. How dare he. And of course all he'd had to do to find the place was ask for The Hollows. She should never have used the name, but she'd been talking about the place she loved most in the world to the man she loved most in the world. She'd been too stupid in love to be cautious.

"Oh, GeeGee, I've done it now." She sighed and prodded her fork into the mass of vegetables and dressing. "How could I know he'd show up on my doorstep?"

It occurred to her suddenly that she could actually ask GeeGee those questions and possibly get an answer. She'd seen her great grandaunt do dozens of séances over the years. She knew how to do them, in addition to scrying in GeeGee's mirrored cup and reading her own tarot. Sure, the process for speaking through the Veil was different when one was by herself versus in a group, but it could easily be done.

She huffed and ate another mouthful of greens. She didn't believe in GeeGee's ghosts. She did believe in the power of suggestion and in developing exquisite cold-reading skills, but those wouldn't help her speak to GeeGee again. GeeGee was beyond the Veil, beyond Delia's reach. Gone.

Sniffling, Delia rubbed her nose with her sleeve, then made herself eat the rest of her salad without thinking anymore. It wasn't easy. Her mind wanted to fixate on what the hell gave Luke the right to walk back into her life after walking out of it six months ago, on what GeeGee would say if they could talk about the situation right now, on whether or not Mom would consent to coming over for the weekend to maybe smooth out some of Delia's ragged edges.

She should be thinking about how to hire someone to pack up her apartment and ship the contents to her. She should be gleefully wording her resignation letter for her shitty job that she hated. She should think about getting a cheap little car to zoom around in now that she had some stability and more than walking distance to the nearest grocery store.

But no. Her mind was full of that bastard Luke.

Even when she finished her dinner, rinsed out the bowl, and placed it in the dishwasher, she couldn't help the churning of her thoughts. The burning injustice of him showing up on her porch. His audacity. How *dare* he.

She stomped up rather than climbing the stairs and flung her clothes off with more irritation than science to take a bath. She needed something calming, but GeeGee knew better than to give her anything lavender-scented. It made her sneeze.

Jasmine again, then. And chamomile. And some Dead Sea salts to soak in. Just what Dr. GeeGee would order if she were here.

Finally, oh finally, she lay in bed, staring up at the dark ceiling, and her mind had settled enough that she could think a little more clearly. She would simply make good on her threat. If Luke showed up again, she would call the police. He hadn't done anything threatening, so she probably couldn't get a restraining order, but GeeGee had been so well-known in the community that she could surely get an officer to drive by and discourage him.

Better. She might be able to sleep now.

The wind chimes jingled distantly, and she smiled softly.

"It's okay, GeeGee. I figured it out."

While she was busy listening for a response, she fell asleep.

13

Delia put her phone to work the next morning, sending Julie a string of texts about Luke's sudden appearance and calling her mother to see if she could come for the weekend.

"If you can't, I totally understand, but I'd feel better if you could."

"Oh, Cordie, of course I can." Mom sounded so soothing that Delia wanted to hug her right then and there, long distance or not. "Don't you worry about a thing. I'll be there for lunch on Saturday, and we can both have ourselves a good cry."

With that settled, Delia flipped back to her texts to see what Julie had said while she was talking. She wasn't disappointed.

> OMG, that absolute coat hanger of a stalker!

> I still can't believe he showed up ON YOUR PORCH! I don't even know how to get there! How did he??

> You know what? You should call the cops and tell them your stalker ex just showed up on your porch, so they should get ready for a restraining order. The NERVE of that asshole!

Then, a few minutes later when Delia obviously hadn't answered back in too long:

> Delia? Answer me right now or I'll assume your stalker ex broke in and murdered you and call the police all the way from California.
>
> Delia, are you listening to me?
>
> DELIA??

Chuckling, she quickly tapped in a suitable response about being on the phone with her mother, for crying out loud, and waited for the three dots to settle again. It didn't take long.

> If I wasn't at work, I'd have already called the police. You can't leave me hanging like that!

Delia sighed, but she was still grinning a little as she typed.

> Sorry. But worry not. Mom's coming for the weekend, so I won't be alone for a couple of days. That should relieve your overprotectiveness.

Julie shot back with a scowly emoji. Delia smirked and typed some more.

> Hey, I like that overprotectiveness. I have no doubt it'll come in handy someday.
>
> You bet your ass it will.
>
> Get back to work, ya slacker. You're a nurse, for god's sake.

She grinned as she started to put her phone aside, then realized the three dots had reappeared. Soon enough, the message popped up.

> I still think you should call the cops. You can't be too careful with a slimeball like Luke.

Delia sighed but didn't answer. She didn't think Luke was a threat to her physical safety—just to her emotional state. She was already such a mess with GeeGee's loss, but to have Luke trying to sleaze his way back into her pants because she had money now?

Gross.

Sighing, she stuffed her phone into the pocket of her old jeans, then went to the cardigans hanging beside the door and picked one. It was still morning-chilly outside, and she wanted to do some gardening. Unfortunately, as soon as she pulled on the knobby old crocheted thing, she got sidetracked, her eyes watering. It smelled like GeeGee.

Closing her eyes tight, she wrapped it around herself and inhaled deeply. Patchouli and fresh air. For a moment, it felt like GeeGee had her arms around her. Delia wished with all her heart that was true.

Swallowing hard, she shook off the latest fit of grief and resolutely walked out the front door and across the porch. The shed was around the side of the house, and she would usually take a little stroll around to see what needed her attention, but right now, she just wanted to work. Anything to take her mind off GeeGee.

Of course, morning gardening wasn't the best way to do that. It felt like her wonderful great grandaunt was just a few rows over as Delia pulled weeds and plied her fork to loosen soil and picked a few things here and there that looked exactly the right ripeness. She had a basketful before she'd looked over all the rows, so she stopped picking and just worked, draping the cardigan over the full basket as she warmed in the rising sunlight.

She wondered again what to do about canning the last of the garden bounty. She couldn't bear for it all to go to waste, and she'd be sad if she didn't have new pickles to choose from come midwinter. GeeGee made the best pickles, and Delia knew where the recipe was kept. She knew where all the recipes were kept. She just didn't know how to can them.

Finally, she finished maintaining the rest of the garden, picked up her basket and her tools, and went to the shed to put the tools away. The basket was heavy, the arching handle digging into her forearm as she lugged it along. She was grateful to heft it up onto the kitchen island, then rub her arm briskly.

Then, she hung the cardigan back on its hook and went upstairs to take a shower. She hadn't exactly worked up a sweat, but she was dirty and very warm from the light exercise, so she wanted to freshen up. She wouldn't bother washing her hair, but she did scrub down the rest of her. Then, she looked at her small assortment of clothes with a frown.

Suddenly, maybe because of that moment with the cardigan, she wanted something of GeeGee's to wear. Was that weird? It might be, but she wasn't sure she cared.

Frowning still, she pulled on her new bra and underwear, wrapped up in her kimono, and went downstairs and down the hallway to her great grandaunt's bedroom. She'd rarely been in this room—usually only as a child in the middle of the night after a nightmare—and she felt like a trespasser. She didn't think she'd ever feel like she really owned this part of the house, no matter how long she lived here. This was GeeGee's place.

And, she thought as she opened up the closet and breathed in the waft of patchouli scent that washed over her, these were GeeGee's things.

The closet was practically its own room. For all that GeeGee was an anti-government hippie flower child, she'd loved her clothes. The walls were lined with racks of clothes arrayed by style and then by color, until she was surrounded by multiple rainbows. Tunic shirts with loose pants. Peasant blouses. Flowy dresses. Broomstick skirts. Baggy sweaters. Colorful patchwork vests. It was all so GeeGee that Delia wanted to cry.

She ran a shaking hand over the nearest line of clothes, deciding against a tunic and pants. She wasn't feeling a broomstick skirt and peasant top, either. Maybe a nice, flowy dress? She wasn't much for dresses usually, but she was sure GeeGee wouldn't mind her borrowing one to see if she liked it now.

Her hand paused halfway through the rainbow of dresses, stopping on a lovely floral pattern on a field of soft green. She pulled the dress out of the mass of fabrics and held it up, eyeing it critically. It was a simple square-necked design with long, flowing sleeves, a high waist, and a full skirt. The flowers were all delicate shades of lilac purple, the green background a mossy sage. She liked it, she decided. Couldn't hurt to put it on, anyway.

She took the dress off the hanger and started to put the hanger back on the rung, only to pause as she saw something through the thin break in the line of clothing. Something... a trunk, maybe? Definitely something low like that. Raising an eyebrow, she slung the chosen dress over one shoulder, then reached out with both hands and shoved the dresses apart.

It *was* a trunk, an old-fashioned wood and metal affair that looked like it could survive an apocalypse. She grinned a little and bent down to see if it was locked. If so, she'd worry about it later, if at all. GeeGee could keep her secrets. She'd literally taken them to the grave, after all.

But that threatened to sink her mood, so she jiggled the latch and was surprised when it opened easily. Not a big secret, then, despite being hidden behind the long dresses in a closet in a private bedroom. Reassured, she opened the top of the trunk and stared down at rows and rows of leather book spines.

No, not books. They were too narrow and uniform for books. Journals, maybe? Diaries? Could that be?

Excited now, though she wondered if perhaps GeeGee would have locked the trunk if she'd known how short her time was, Delia finagled a slim volume out of the middle and looked at the cover. The numbers 2004 glowed in embossed gold on the brown leather. It *was* a diary or a journal.

Should she? Biting her lower lip, she put the selected book back in place, then decided to get dressed while she thought about it. She shucked out of her kimono and hurried to pull the green and lilac dress over her head. She and GeeGee were about the same size now that Delia had lost weight—though GeeGee had lost a little of her height in the last decade or so—so the dress was a good fit. The hem went down to her ankles and the sleeves fluttered around her wrists. She felt… dainty. She wasn't used to feeling dainty.

She liked it, she thought. She hadn't worn a dress since she was a teenager.

And she decided to take the first volume over to GeeGee's armchair and just skim a little. See how personal the writing was. If it looked like something GeeGee would want to keep a secret, Delia would just put it back in the trunk and forget the diaries existed.

Resolved, she reached into the back left-hand corner and worked what she assumed was the first year's journal out of its accustomed place. It didn't want to come out, but she managed. 1981. Delia hadn't even been born yet. It seemed like an impossibly long time ago.

Grinning a little, though she felt like someone would catch her and get her in big trouble, she walked over to the old wing-back chair and sat down with one leg tucked up under her. Surely GeeGee wouldn't mind if she took one little peek. She'd put it back if it looked too private, she reminded herself as she opened the front cover.

The pages were printed with each day's date, but GeeGee's handwriting didn't begin until almost halfway through the year. Delia flipped to the first entry, then started reading the tidy print.

> *I remember all of them, you see. Every last one. Twenty-three, at this point, but I suspect I'm not done yet.*

Delia raised an eyebrow. It was a strange way to start a diary, she thought. Twenty-three what?

> *There's a name for what I am, it seems. I found it reading The New York Times just yesterday. There's a man from Atlanta who is very like me, I believe. Wayne Williams.*

A strange feeling crept up the back of her neck. Something was wrong about this, and not just reading someone else's private thoughts. Who was this Wayne Williams guy? And what did he have to do with GeeGee?

> *A serial killer.*

Eyes widening, Delia read faster, not believing what she was seeing. It was a joke. GeeGee's weird sense of humor.

> *I quite like the sound of that. It has a certain grandeur we women are often denied.*

She slammed the book closed and stood up so fast out of the chair that she almost fell over. She shouldn't have peeked. Maybe this was GeeGee's way of making sure no one ever read her diaries. It had to be a joke. GeeGee's legendary sense of humor, but... twisted somehow.

Twisted and not actually funny.

Heart racing, Delia put the volume back in the trunk and closed it, then pulled the dresses back into place to hide it. She shouldn't have peeked. She deserved to get pranked from beyond the grave for reading GeeGee's diary.

That's all it was. A prank.

That's all.

14

Delia didn't sleep well that night. It took forever to fall asleep, and it was a thin scrim at best. She woke up several times, convinced she heard someone moving in the house, but when she sat up in the dark and listened, she heard nothing. Not even the creak of the house settling or the dim jingling of the wind chimes. Was someone or something really moving?

At 2:00 AM, it was easy to think maybe GeeGee had come back to get revenge on her for reading her diary. Silliness, of course, but she'd learned that at 2:00 AM, everything seemed rational.

When she finally dragged out of bed just after dawn, she felt like she'd slept on a mattress full of rocks, her body achy from all the tossing and turning. She threw on her dirty old jeans for another morning gardening stint, made a joyless breakfast of muesli from a cabinet and the last bit of milk, and pulled on a cardigan with less nostalgia than she'd felt yesterday. She perked up a little in the good morning sunlight, but she still went at the weeding and picking with less vigor than she should probably feel.

When her basket was full and her old jeans were dirtier still, she put away her tools and went back inside, only then remembering she was supposed to be back at work today.

Oops.

Oh, well. She was planning to quit without going back anyway, though she hadn't planned on quitting without *any* notice. She'd just... been distracted. With everything.

Sighing, she sorted out the produce on the kitchen island, leaving everything she wanted to put on her salad in the middle and moving everything else off to one side, then pulled out her phone. Better to make the break now while she was thinking about it. She scrolled to her boss's number and called.

"You were supposed to be at work this morning."

Well. There was a fine hello. She decided to answer in kind.

"Sorry, Mr. Delgado, but I actually quit like two days ago and just forgot to call you."

"I'm sorry?"

She sighed. "No, I'm sorry. I didn't mean to bite. I'm not coming back to California. I'm staying in Missouri. I meant to call but got sidetracked with all the bereavement issues here."

"That is no excuse. I hope you know you'll never get a good reference from this company, Miss Jameson."

She very nearly snorted but caught herself. "I'm well aware, Mr. Delgado. It can't be helped. Goodbye."

"What am I supposed to do about your—"

She hung up with more satisfaction than she'd felt all morning. She was still grinning when she climbed out of the shower and dried her hair, in fact. For a while, she forgot about her little foray into GeeGee's closet. She put on her own clothes, though. No more poking around in GeeGee's things. Not for a good, long while. If she wanted a dress, she'd just have to buy one.

But before she started online shopping, she decided to flop onto her bed and Google around California for moving firms that would pack up an apartment and ship it. To her surprise, she found several and was able to bargain shop for the one she wanted. She wouldn't have her things for almost two weeks, but she couldn't argue with the price or the convenience.

No more California. Now if she could just get Luke to go back there, she'd be set. Well, if she could convince Julie to move to Missouri....

Unfortunately, that would never happen. Julie was a pediatric nurse who loved both her job and the hospital she worked for. Well, the kids she worked for. No way would she up and move away on a whim.

Grinning at the thought, Delia strolled down the stairs to make herself some lunch, then paused just inside the kitchen. Hadn't she sorted everything out on the island? She could've sworn she'd at least taken everything out of the basket.

But there the basket stood on the island, heaped full of fresh-from-the-garden produce that she'd picked herself.

She frowned. She thought she'd at least put aside the cherry tomatoes and cucumbers and some carrots. She may have left everything else, but she was almost sure she'd....

She looked around the kitchen as if expecting to see someone standing in the corner, but of course, there was no one. She was alone in the house. And no, GeeGee hadn't come back from the grave to freak her out by re-packing the produce.

Snorting at herself, she shook off her unease and busied herself with sorting out the produce—possibly again—and deciding what she wanted in her salad. She'd been surprised to see green leaf lettuce, spinach, and arugula still growing. She was even able to pull some baby kale, though most of it had grown full-sized this late in the season. She knew GeeGee had a way of frequently sowing new seeds to continue the harvest through the fall, but she'd never learned how. She supposed she'd have to now if she wanted to keep having salads without going to the store for the green leafies.

Soon enough, she had one of the big salad bowls full up with vegetable goodness and some good, strong balsamic vinaigrette over the lot. She'd even found some fake bacon bits, likely left over from one of GeeGee's little gatherings with her witchy friends who were, more often than not, vegetarians or even vegan. GeeGee was practically a vegetarian herself, but she liked ham and eggs too much to go full vegan. And real bacon. Who didn't like real bacon?

Smiling at the memory of many a huge, baked, honey-glazed, bone-in ham with roasted potatoes and turnips and carrots, Delia took her lunch to the window nook and sat down at the little table with a glass of iced tea. It was really too chilly for iced tea. She should make herself a pot of hot tea for reading this afternoon.

She supposed she could buy the latest MMORPG and get sucked in, now that she didn't have to go to work anymore, but most of her old guild friends had moved on without her as she had to work more and more hours. She missed too many raids, she supposed. She'd have to make all new online friends if she wanted to play.

Just another thing she'd let California take away from her, she supposed, along with her dream of creating her own game.

No, she corrected herself. Not California. Just the job and, eventually, Luke. He hadn't liked her spending so much time on something that wasn't him. And he'd been suspicious of her online friends. He constantly asked how many were men, how many had asked her out, how many had her cell number.

Red flags. He was just a walking bouquet of red flags, and she hadn't seen them. Not until it was too late.

She poked at her salad and hoped he'd take her advice and leave. She did not want him hanging around, trying to get back into her good graces. She did not want to have to learn how to take out a restraining order.

And, if she was honest, she didn't want to fall back in with him and wasn't sure how strong her resolve to stay free would be against a determined onslaught of his twisted charm.

She looked out the window as the wind chimes jingled gently. The stretch of garden outside looked lovely, even this late in the year. GeeGee, of course, knew how to stagger her plants' growing cycles so that something was blooming from earliest spring to latest reach of autumn. She'd even planted evergreens like yew, rowan, barberry, and holly to continue having bright spots of color on the trees year-round.

Another thing Delia would have to learn. She knew a little, of course, from endless conversations with GeeGee while they weeded and picked and hoed, but unless GeeGee had written down all the little tricks of the trade, Delia might have to invest in a landscaper to come help her with it all. The yard wasn't as large as, say, a golf course, but almost all of it had flowers or shrubs or ornamental indigenous grasses—literally anything besides mowable grass—including bits that were terraced with natural stone or railroad ties.

And the koi pond, of course. She'd need some help taking care of the little waterfall fountain implement that kept the water fresh and moving. It was getting late in the year. Did she have to take the fish out for the winter?

So much to do now. So much to know. However would she get it all done? She smirked at the windows. Oh, right, she didn't have a job. That's how she'd get it all done.

Her phone chimed, and she looked down to see who it was. Unknown number. She rolled her eyes and prepared to be very annoyed with Luke for trying with yet another number.

Then, she paused. The message looked strange. Was it really just... a *HI?*

Frowning, she tapped in her code—she'd never trusted the thumbprint reader—and opened the message and, yes, it really was just a *HI*. No punctuation or anything. Who would send her just a *HI?*

Good grief, what sort of ploy was this now? She wouldn't have thought Luke could do anything more unexpected than showing up on her porch, but she couldn't have predicted this one. Why? It was just bizarre.

Shaking her head, she swiped to delete the message, then paused and tapped on it instead to block the number. She wondered wearily how many numbers she'd have to block now that she was an heiress with a greedy ex.

Too many, she thought, finishing her salad and taking the bowl to the sink to rinse. Too damn many.

Maybe she should just change her number.

Tempting. Very tempting.

15

Early in the afternoon, Delia pulled on one of GeeGee's floppy, straw sun hats and her own sunglasses, stepped out onto the porch, and took a deep breath. She had an errand to run, but not one she needed a car for. At least, not yet. A duty visit, as GeeGee might say.

Squaring her shoulders, she trotted down the porch's steps and took off across the yard to the driveway, then kept right on walking. The drive was a twisty thing, a quarter of a mile as the crow flies but much longer with all the turns that allowed the trees to hide the house from the main road, and uphill all the way out of the aptly named Hollows. She'd taken this walk many a time as a child and a youth, but she'd become too used to sitting behind a desk these past five years. By the time she finally reached the end of the driveway, she was exhausted, and she still had another quarter of a mile to go.

Mr. Brinkley's property abutted GeeGee's—hers—but their houses were both toward the middle of their spreads, so the distance between them seemed a lot farther than it was. She worked up a light sweat walking on the shoulder of the two-lane road that fronted both properties and hoped she didn't smell by the time she'd turned off the main road and into her neighbor's driveway.

If she walked the opposite way—which she had no intention of doing—she'd have about the same distance to go to the next driveway, but she was pretty sure that place was still empty. If she remembered correctly, the sweet old gal who'd owned it when she was a kid died a couple of years back, and some nephew owned it now. GeeGee said something once about him hating the country, so he'd apparently put it up for sale and left it to rot.

Such a shame. The old lady, Gladys Something-or-other, had been so kind and made the best apple cobbler Delia had ever eaten. Especially fresh from the oven with a dollop of vanilla ice cream melting into all the nooks and crannies.

But this was Mr. Brinkley's rather boring house she walked up to, puffing and trying to hide it, and while he was a good neighbor, he tended to be a bit... brusque. A man of few words, as it were.

She slowed down as she approached, thinking to herself that GeeGee's house always struck her as vaguely magical in appearance, but Mr. Brinkley's four-square farmhouse was just as down to earth as a house could be without being a literal box. She admitted to herself that she hadn't really slowed down to judge the house and its owner but to catch her breath a little before having to talk. She'd really fallen out of shape with her sit-down office job.

Before she could fully recover, Mr. Brinkley threw open his screen door and stepped out onto his wrap-around porch, tipping his hat to her.

"Ms. Jameson."

"Mr. Brinkley," she said, trying not to sound winded. "I thought I ought to come over and see if there was anything

GeeGee did that you wanted to go over with me. Maybe something I might forget to take care of, being a new homeowner."

He nodded, flinty gray eyes studying her, possibly judging her. "Come on in. Just made some iced tea."

She nodded, too, and followed him into the blocky, dim house, weaving through the old-timey furniture back to the kitchen. He gestured for her to sit at the heavy, hardwood farm table as he went to the fridge.

"Was glad to hear you'd come down." He pulled down two tall, heavy glasses from a cabinet and placed them, one at a time, under the ice maker in the fridge door. "Sorry you missed the funeral, though."

Delia winced. "Me, too. It felt so wrong, but I couldn't get off work. It was... so sudden."

Mr. Brinkley nodded. "She understood." He scuffed his booted feet across the linoleum to the table and plunked down the glasses, then plunked himself down into a seat catty-corner from her. "Some of the relatives might not, but Miss Virginia did."

Her eyes watered. This was one reason she'd put off this visit longer than was really polite. The commiserating. The remembering. She already did too much of that as it was.

"Thank you, Mr. Brinkley."

"Just Don."

Her eyes widened, but she nodded. "And I'm Delia."

Absurdly, he reached a hand out to her, as if they'd never met before. She supposed they hadn't, really. She'd been so much younger the last time she saw him.

So, smiling softly, her eyes still stinging with the start of tears, she took the offered hand for a good, solid shake.

"Well, Miss Delia, there ain't much you need to know right now about the place. I'll come help you winter some of the plants after the first hard frost, but it's mostly just harvesting the rest of the garden for now. Maybe turn over the compost bins if you have the inclination before winter sets in."

"What about the koi pond?"

He shrugged. "The fish are already eating the cold weather food, so just keep feeding them from the green barrel instead of the blue one."

Cold weather food? She supposed that made sense. The fish sort of... hibernated?... in winter, so they'd want to fatten up before then. She thought. Maybe.

"Once it starts frosting over at night, you'll wanna check your thermometer every morning. Once it stays below fifty degrees or so, you'll wanna stop feeding altogether." He scratched behind one big ear. "I don't rightly remember whether Miss Virginia put the net up yet or not, but you'll want that up as soon as possible to keep leaf litter out of the pool so it don't get slimy."

She tried not to look as dumb as she felt. "Net?"

"I'll show you. You'd have noticed it if it was already up. It's like a tent, but with netting instead of canvas." He nodded sagely. "I'll help you winterize the water plants once it's time, but we have some time left before then. Then, it's just shutting down the waterfall and waiting for spring thaw. The aerator will do the rest."

She didn't know what an aerator was. She also didn't know how to shut down the waterfall. Was there a switch? Would it be easy to find?

He chuckled suddenly, his face collapsing from its usual morose, slightly stern look into a mass of jolly wrinkles. He went from miser to Santa in the blink of a twinkling gray eye.

"I'll help, Miss Delia. I especially wouldn't make you do it alone this first winter. It'll be old hat by the time next winter comes around."

Relief flooded her and she huffed slightly, not quite up to laughing.

"Come spring, you won't have to worry none about mowing. Miss Virginia didn't hold with that golf course crap, so most of the low-growing greenery in the yard is clover and creeping thyme, hens and chickens, that sort of thing. Nothing that grows high enough to need mowing."

That, she'd known and was grateful for. She'd hated Mom's old push mower as a kid. It weighed a ton and was balky as hell. She never used it without ending up with blisters and an aching back.

"The property itself shouldn't need any major work unless a tree comes down. If it's not in the driveway, it'll keep until spring unless you just need firewood, but Miss Virginia already had a fellow over on the other side of town lay in a supply at the end of summer. It needs to dry out before you use it, ya know."

Delia didn't know that, but again, she supposed it made sense. And it was a relief to know she wouldn't have to learn to use a chainsaw. Although she might need a refresher course on how to use the fireplace in the living room when it started getting really cold. She didn't want to burn GeeGee's beloved house down.

"Is there anything else you wanted to know?"

She considered, her head already feeling full of all the things to do. Then, she brightened.

"Any idea where I could get a relatively cheap used farm truck?"

Patricia the Uber driver might want a Cooper, but Delia was a farm truck sort of girl. She might have liked wearing GeeGee's dress, but she'd always be a jeans and t-shirt woman when she didn't want to look elegant.

Besides, an old farm truck was what GeeGee used to have before she gave up driving. It seemed right somehow.

Don rubbed his scrubby chin. "I reckon my nephew could get you a deal on one from that lot he works at down on Lockwood. Don't let him talk you into anything foreign, now."

She hid a grin. She'd be looking at gas mileage and longevity more than location of manufacture, but he didn't need to know that.

"What's the name of the place?"

He stood up from the table, and she took a moment to take a few gulps of her iced tea. A little too sweet, she thought, but refreshing and cool, just the same.

"I got a card here somewhere. Ah, here we go." He came back to the table and handed her a little business card that she pocketed. "Tell him his uncle sent you. He'll treat you right."

"Thanks, Don." She smiled. "I can't tell you how glad I am that you were here...."

He started to wave her off, then just nodded instead. "She was the best neighbor I ever had, was Miss Virginia." He tilted his head to one side. "Into the occult a little, but a shrewd woman other than that."

Again, she wanted to grin, but she kept her warm smile on instead. "That she was."

They were quiet for a moment, sipping their tea, and then Delia realized it was time to go. She'd gotten most of the information she'd come for and had earned a promise of help, should she need it. She was all set, so she stood up.

"Well, I have to get back, but I want to thank you for the help."

This, he did wave off. "No problem at all, Miss Delia. You take care of yourself, now, and call if you need something quick-like."

"Will do." She reached out for another shake, which he gave with a craggy grin. "Goodbye, Don."

He tipped two fingers to his forehead, which she took as a return goodbye. When she was back out in the fresh air, she realized that his place smelled like old people and abruptly wondered why GeeGee's house didn't smell like that.

"It's the patchouli," she said out loud, then looked back to make sure Mr. Brinkley hadn't come outside to see her off, only to catch her talking to herself.

Luckily, he'd stayed inside, and she was able to make her escape unscathed, her dignity mostly still intact. She counted it a win.

16

Delia couldn't get comfortable on the couch in the parlor. She'd been trying to read, lying down with a soothing pot of tea steaming away at her elbow on the coffee table, for a good hour now, but she couldn't get comfortable. She felt antsy, and she didn't know why.

I quite like the sound of that.

IT SOUNDED AS IF GEEGEE HAD SPOKEN OUT LOUD IN THE ROOM, so real was the thought. The memory, if she was being honest.

That's why she couldn't settle. The back of her mind was gnawing on the bone that was GeeGee's first diary entry.

Which was stupid because it was just a stupid joke.

If it's a joke, she wouldn't mind me reading more. But Delia quashed that thought before it could fully form, because she wasn't reading any more of that diary, and that was final.

She shifted on the usually comfortable couch, not able to

hold her book exactly where she wanted it, for some reason. Her wrist was tired. Her neck ached. Her head felt hot and full. She was hungry.

Except it wasn't really any of those things, and she put the book aside with a heavy sigh.

"It's just a stupid joke." Maybe if she said it out loud, she'd believe it and get over the curiosity nipping at the back of her brain. "It's the equivalent of the curses on ancient Egyptian tombs. That's all. Power of suggestion. A mind fuck, to put it bluntly. GeeGee was great at those."

She took a sip of tea, some chamomile herbal blend with honey for extra soothing power, and tried to get her brain to be rational. GeeGee wasn't a serial killer. The entire thought was ludicrous. The woman had adopted countless Feed the Children kids over the years. She wore all natural fibers and had sourced as much of her house responsibly as she possibly could in Missouri. She grew and canned her own produce and did séances in her parlor and chatted with her lady friends and went on lovely vacations at least twice a year. She was a goddamn hippie, as her own father used to say, only somewhat fondly.

GeeGee was a saint, not a serial killer.

So why did it bother her so much?

"Ugh. Just go read some more and find out what the joke is. Enough, already."

Sighing dramatically, she flung herself up out of the couch and trudged to GeeGee's bedroom, looking at the closet doors with distaste. She would read the entire first entry and be done with it. Get it off her mind. That's all.

Setting her shoulders, she opened the door, turned on the light, pushed back the dresses, and looked down at the chest. She should have locked it, making this a moot point, but she hadn't. She knew, she supposed. She knew she wouldn't be able to leave it alone for long.

Grumbling under her breath all the while, she worked the first volume out of its place in the back corner, took it over to the wingback, and sat down, both feet firmly on the floor. She looked down at the shiny gold 1981 on the leather cover, then opened it up and flipped to the first entry. Shaking her head, she read it again.

I remember all of them, you see. Every last one. Twenty-three, at this point, but I suspect I'm not done yet.

There's a name for what I am, it seems. I found it reading The New York Times just yesterday. There's a man from Atlanta who is very like me, I believe. Wayne Williams.

A serial killer.

I quite like the sound of that. It has a certain grandeur we women are often denied. A gender neutrality that so few labels imply.

It's a relief to have a label that defines me without restricting me to a submissive role. One that makes me not so... wrong. Oh, of course it's wrong to kill people, but there are others like me. Others who feel this need inside them, burning to be set free. That means it's not a problem but a <u>human condition</u>, and I am once again a member of the human race.

I've often wondered, you see, though I'm not one of those people incapable of love or other genuine emotion. I feel things like I suppose anyone does. I love my mother and brother, niece and nephews, friends, pets over the years. I've felt desire with men and hatred of the same. I get angry and I get happy. I'm not an empty vessel.

But that is perhaps the real tragedy of what I am. I <u>feel</u>. I feel... regret. Shame. Determination.

Yes, that. Determination. I won't be stopped, you see. I can't.

My work is not yet done.

SKIN CRAWLING, DELIA CLOSED THE BOOK WITHOUT SLAMMING IT this time, then just sat in the wingback, staring off into space, seeing nothing. Feeling nothing emotionally. It was too soon yet to feel.

That didn't sound like a joke. Not at all. That sounded like insight. Like the personal thoughts of someone grasping at a life preserver in a turbulent sea.

She shouldn't have read further. If only she could've kept telling herself that it was all one big joke, one big DO NOT ENTER sign on GeeGee's secrets. If only she could take it all back.

Because Delia believed it. She couldn't work her mind around it yet, but she couldn't deny the raw honesty in those neatly written words. There was no dithering in those tidy lines of easily readable text. There was surety. There was... relief.

Her stomach lurched, and she tossed the diary onto the bed as she jumped out of the chair and ran for GeeGee's bathroom. She threw up everything she'd eaten all day, then hovered, still kneeling, over the toilet, waiting to see if she was done. Another lurch, but no vomit. She spat into the toilet, worked up some more saliva, spat again.

The smell floating up from the water threatened to set her off again, so she stood up on shaky legs and flushed, turning to the sink to rinse her mouth out with water from the tap.

"Fuck," she said out loud and cupped handfuls of cold water to splash on her face. "Fucking hell."

She dragged her wet hands through her hair, hauling it back from her face, then wiped off with the nearest hand towel. When she felt vaguely all right again, she looked at herself in the mirror and felt that semblance of normality blow away like a fart in a high wind.

She looked shocked to death. Her face was translucently pale with dark patches under her wide eyes. It was even worse, somehow, with her wet hair plastered back from her face. She looked like a corpse on an autopsy table in a morgue. All she needed was fluorescent lighting to complete the effect.

"Jesus," she said. "Jesus Christ."

GeeGee, the touchstone of her life, her solid rock in the storm. It didn't compute. Her mind edged up to the fact, then shied away in horror. It couldn't be true.

But it definitely wasn't a joke.

"Enough." She was practically panting, her voice almost a moan. "Enough for tonight. Please."

She closed her eyes. The image of black-printed handwriting on white pages tried to scroll past, but she refused. She couldn't bear it. She couldn't think about it any more right now.

"Tomorrow." She clenched her teeth, then forced herself to relax her jaw. "I will think about it tomorrow, because tomorrow is another day."

Jesus. She must be hurting if she was sampling from *Gone with the Wind*.

The thought didn't get even a hint of a chuckle. The movie had always been a bone of contention between Delia and her mother, with Mom saying it was one of the greatest movies of all time and Delia declaring it boring and being glad at the end that practically everyone died.

But there was no comfort to be had today. No shelter from what she'd accidentally found.

And it was all her own damn fault.

Sighing heavily, seemingly from the soles of her feet, she pushed away from the vanity, shut off the light, and walked right past the diary on the bed. It really was enough for tonight. She simply couldn't bear any more revelations.

17

There was no sleep that night. Delia tossed and turned, rearranged her covers, fluffed her pillows, stared up at the dark ceiling, and all for naught. Her mind was too full of thoughts. Of contradictions. Of revelations.

The worst thought of all, though, was how could GeeGee do this to her?

It was a stupid thought and made no sense. GeeGee hadn't done anything at all to Delia. GeeGee had, in fact, left her a fortune and encouraged her to be like Sinatra and live life her way. But the thought persisted. She couldn't shake it. How could GeeGee *do* this to her?

A serial killer. She still balked at the thought. It couldn't be true. It simply couldn't. GeeGee was old. GeeGee was kind and generous. GeeGee was *old*.

But she hadn't been old in 1981, Delia reminded herself. She didn't know what age Virginia Falkirk had been in 1981, but it certainly hadn't been old. Forty, maybe? Late thirties? Definitely not withered with age.

Twenty-three. The number was impossible. There was simply no earthly way that GeeGee—Delia's GeeGee—had killed twenty-three people. In her entire life, let alone in the first thirty or forty years of it.

But that awful thought spawned another one that had her sitting up in bed and blinking into the dark. What if... what if there were more?

The diary had said she wasn't done. What if there were more since then?

And how, for fuck's sake? How could GeeGee be a fucking serial killer, and no one knew?

Delia flung herself back onto her pillow, throwing her arms out wide. It was impossible. It was all completely, unthinkably impossible.

Grumbling under her breath, she sat back up, threw aside the covers, and climbed out of bed. She had to know more. She couldn't sleep like this. She needed to read more and figure out... how. How any of this was reality.

She needed... an explanation. Something that would fit this new, strange-shaped piece of information into her world view. Surely, somewhere in all those volumes, was an answer to all the questions she didn't even know how to ask herself.

She didn't bother putting on her kimono over her long-sleeved t-shirt and flannel pajama pants. She did, however, pull on a thick pair of socks. The hardwoods were cold.

Soon enough, she headed downstairs, hesitated in the foyer, then detoured to the kitchen to make herself a pot of tea. She wouldn't be able to sleep tonight, anyway, so she might as well be warm and comforted while she dipped her toe into impossible madness.

By the time she finally settled into the wingback chair with the year 1981 in hand and a steaming, dainty, flowered cup of Earl Grey near at hand, Delia felt more determination than anything else. She would figure out what the hell was going on. She would prove... well, she didn't know what, but she would by god do it anyway.

Opening the diary, she flipped to the second entry and started reading, a grimace on her face.

I may well have shocked the librarian in town. I didn't ask for her help finding books on murder, but she did have to check them out for me. I've only ever borrowed romances, mysteries, and gardening books before now, and while there's a fair bit of murder to be had in a mystery, these books are nonfiction and, I must admit, quite grisly.

Did you know, for instance, that a man named H.H. Holmes built a murder hotel back in the 1890s? It is fabulously gruesome. Built-in torture and gas chambers. And he sold his victims' bodies as cadavers to medical schools.

DELIA ROLLED HER EYES, FEELING ABSURDLY RELIEVED. Obviously, none of that was true. It was all yellow journalism from the time and had long since been debunked. At best, Holmes—which wasn't even his real name—killed a couple of people out of what could be called necessity, not bloodlust or psychological need.

Maybe GeeGee was pulling her leg via time-travel, after all. Smiling a little, albeit wryly, Delia read on.

And there's Jack the Ripper, of course. One of the most famous of all, though he only had the five known victims. But the audacity of the crimes, the defiling of the bodies... that's what set him apart. I've read so much about him, but honestly, I feel he's overrated.

Of far more interest to me was Elizabeth Bathory, who supposedly killed peasant girls and bathed in their blood to keep her youthful appearance. A veritable vampire, that one, and far more prolific than either Holmes or ol' Jack.

I rather feel a kinship with her, though I've never taken a woman. I would never. We women must stick together in this world, and we have a far greater adversary than we could ever be to each other, Lady Bathory excluded. MEN.

Pausing, Delia reached for her cup of tea and took a drink with a surprisingly steady hand. She'd expected to be trembling with rage or fear or astonishment by now, but instead, she was... absorbed.

If nothing else, GeeGee was an engaging writer. Too bad she'd never written a book.

I have only ever taken the most obvious and oblivious of prey: the straight, white man. I could never harm a child or an animal, though I've read that harming animals is one of the signals of my kind. I would never harm another woman or someone society considers lesser than—the crippled, the black folk, the Indians, the gays, the sex slaves working out on the street. I hold these wonderful people up, fight for them. I could never harm them.

But straight, white men? They sicken me. I am often asked when will I settle down, when will I marry, when will I have children and live a good, Christian life. It's all I can do not to laugh in their faces. I would far rather kill a man than marry him.

And have done.

Tension wormed its way up Delia's spine. That didn't sound like a travelog of serial killers of the past, as had the earlier segment. That sounded... angry. Angry enough to make Delia worry all over again that maybe any of this was true, after all.

But I digress. I was talking about my research into my kind. I shouldn't feel the need to justify my choice of prey, but as I said before, my sense of guilt is perfectly well developed, and it cries out for explanation, for justification. Men deserve what I bring to them, but still, I feel the need to defend myself.

It doesn't escape my notice that most of this so-called history of serial killers is of men. Rodney Alcala, that man who was on The Dating Game and won. Ed Gein, who did such unspeakable things to his victims and their corpses. David Berkowitz, the Son of Sam himself. Ed Kemper, who knew himself well enough to know he couldn't be free. William Bonin, the Freeway Killer. John Wayne Gacy, the killer clown with his handcuff trick. Ted Bundy, who raped and murdered all those poor young women.

Yes, the Ted Bundy and John Wayne Gacy and Ed Gein types are, I fear, the worst of my lot. They make me despair. They inflict such misery and torture on their victims, raping, defiling....

I am not like that. I have no urge to toy with my prey. I simply want it to cease to be.

Was it a sign of just how upset Delia was about this entire subject that she was relieved by that last bit? She hadn't thought it through nearly far enough to think about her beloved great grandaunt raping her way through twenty-three victims, but apparently, that wasn't the case. It was not a relief she expected, but she'd fucking take it.

The follow up line, "I simply want it to cease to be," removed some of that surprising comfort, though. Jesus.

There are such horrors amongst us human beings, but I still am, to my relief and as I said before, human. And, I feel, more human than these awful men who commit such atrocities on weaker prey, on those who are already amongst the downtrodden.

A justification? Or a false dichotomy? Can I make an accurate judgment of myself when I, too, am guilty of the only truly unforgivable sin?

Or is that the lapsed Christian in me?

I can't know the answer to that. It's too soon.

More research. To be continued.

Delia closed the book, using her finger to mark the page, and rubbed her eyes. They were gritty from reading with just a lamp's light and lack of sleep. But mostly, she rubbed her eyes because she wanted to cry. The words were so stark, so inarguable, so... wise and introspective.

Yes, that was the truly awful part. GeeGee was, like anyone else keeping a diary, trying to understand herself, and it was horrendous. Terrible. So, so troubling.

This time, her hand was shaking as she reached for her teacup. How could she begin to integrate all of this with what she knew of the woman who had been there for her from her earliest memory? Who was her second home? Who had just left her a goddamn fortune and a whole new life?

Jesus, could she even accept the money, knowing who it came from? The monster who had amassed it? What if it hadn't been canny investing and hard work that had raised GeeGee's fortune, after all? What if *this* had somehow earned it?

The world spun around her, but Delia had never felt less like passing out than right now. No, she felt widely, futilely awake. She felt as if she'd never sleep again. Every horrible question raised a dozen others until it felt like she was standing on quicksand instead of *terra firma*.

"GeeGee," she all but moaned, "what have you done? How could you?"

Dimly, like a hint of a far away dream, she heard the gentle jingle of the wind chimes on the patio. She felt suddenly cold, but the only warm thing around was either the quilt off GeeGee's bed or the thick robe hanging on the back of GeeGee's door. Delia didn't think she could handle that patchouli scent right now. It would be cloying, choking, and not comforting at all.

She'd just stay cold, thanks.

But she pulled her socked feet up off the chilly floor and curled up in the chair, the diary against her chest. She shuddered. She didn't want it touching her, but she couldn't hold onto it otherwise, and she didn't think she was done reading yet.

So thinking, she fell asleep, her grip loosening until the diary fell to the floor.

It didn't awaken her. She was too far gone.

18

Delia's neck hurt. So did her back. And she was cold. Why was she so cold?

She blinked her eyes open, then looked around blearily, unsure where the hell she was. Nothing looked familiar. She was....

GeeGee's room. Diary. Serial killer.

Groaning, she uncurled from the now-uncomfortable chair, only to step on the diary and crease some of the pages. She shouldn't care. It was the diary of a madwoman.

But she discovered that she did care, so she reached down and picked it up, unfolding the pages so she could shut the diary properly. She got up painfully and hobble-stepped over to the bed to put it down gently. Her tea things took up too much of the end table by the wingback. There simply wasn't room for one more thing.

Then, she stretched and groaned out loud, really letting loose. A loud creak out in the main area of the house made her jump, almost throwing out her back with the sudden change. What the hell was that? It sounded like… maybe the stairs settling? Very loudly?

She'd only ever heard that sort of sound when she or GeeGee was walking around upstairs. Was... Jesus, was someone in the house? She hadn't been locking the door because this was the country, but she definitely should have been, especially with Luke showing up out of nowhere. Jesus, why hadn't she been locking her door?

Cold all over suddenly, she stood, indecisive. What should she do? Call the police? But her phone was upstairs, and that was likely where the invader was. Go look?

What would GeeGee—not serial killer GeeGee, but the amazing, strong woman she'd grown up admiring—do?

Straightening her shoulders, Delia gritted her teeth and tiptoed to the door, glad she was wearing socks so she could sneak up on whoever it was. Unfortunately, most of the floor between here and the upstairs was hardwood, so if it came down to a chase, she'd be at a disadvantage as she slipped and slid everywhere, but she couldn't do anything about that now. She'd take being silent over being fast. But she needed a weapon. Something to defend herself with.

Another creak sounded through the silence, so she settled her hand on the doorknob to turn it as slowly as she could. She didn't remember it ever making noise before, but she'd never tried to be silent before, either. The door opened with the slightest of squeaks, and she slipped out into the hall, then up it to where the foyer joined with the rest of the house. There, she hesitated. What would work as a weapon?

The kitchen. GeeGee's block of huge kitchen knives. That should do the trick. Could she get there and back without making a sound? She thought so. The kitchen floor was tile and much less likely to creak and give her away than all the hardwood.

She headed off that way and picked up the biggest knife that would fit easily in her hand—she was tempted to take the big chopper, but she wanted something with a point—then turned back toward the foyer and the staircase. She was doing this. She was going upstairs where someone might be lurking.

Heart throbbing in her throat, she crept up the first couple of steps, then remembered something about stairs being less likely to creak if she walked to either side instead of up the middle. She had no idea if that was true or not, but she thought it couldn't hurt to huddle next to the wall as she made her way up. It felt more secure to have something at her side, anyway. More protected. Nothing could sneak up to her that way, anyway, so she could focus on looking up and ahead.

Unfortunately, she saw nothing as she reached the landing. Which way should she go first? Toward the office, or toward her own room? Would someone break in to maybe steal something from the office, or were they here for her? Who even knew she was here besides her own lawyer and money guy?

And Luke. And Elijah Campbell. Hell, she even threw in Patricia the Uber driver for the hell of it.

Biting at her lower lip, she forwent the office and headed toward her own room. She'd look it over first. Surely, no one was here for her. If anyone was here at all, they were surely here for money or valuables, and the only valuables in her room were a TV and a computer gaming system, which would be too cumbersome to haul out by just one person.

The floor creaked under her socked foot, and she froze, swallowing down a groan, the knife suddenly feeling slick in her sweaty grip. She heard… something. A flurry of quiet movement, a sliding sort of sound. Someone was in her room. Someone was in her *room*.

Cold all over, except in her sweaty palms, she clenched her teeth and debated just running downstairs, out of the house, down the driveway, and over to Mr. Brinkley's place to have him call the cops. That might be the smart thing to do.

But that's not what GeeGee would do, and, current diary

situation notwithstanding, Delia had never gone wrong following GeeGee's advice.

She advanced.

Five steps. Ten. Twenty, and there was her door, just in reach. Silence from within her room now. She closed her eyes for a second, girding up her will, then reached out and touched the doorknob. She'd have to be fast, have whatever element of surprise remained after that creak gave her away.

She flung the door open and ran inside, the knife raised up by her ear. The room... was empty.

The window. The window was open, the screen kicked out, the curtains blowing gently inward, billowing in the cold morning breeze.

The intruder was gone.

19

"There's some crushed grass under the window where he landed and rolled, Miss Jameson, and some footprints in the frost running off toward the woods that-a-way, but we lost the track at the stream." The cop pushed back his trooper hat and scratched his forehead. "Coulda gone anywhere from there. Sorry to say, ma'am, but we lost him."

Her lips feeling numb, despite the cardigan she'd wrapped around herself, Delia murmured half under her breath, "How sure are you that it's a man?"

"What's that, ma'am?"

"Sorry." She shook herself and raised her voice to a more normal tone. "I was just saying it might not be a man."

He shrugged. "That's true enough, but I don't think so. If it's a woman, she has one hell of a long stride."

It was GeeGee she was thinking of, of course. GeeGee, who had killed twenty-three people—twenty-three *men*—and apparently hadn't been caught.

"Anyway, Miss Jameson, we'll file a full report when we get back to town, and if you have any more trouble, you give us a call. Is there anyone we should be aware of? Anyone who knows you're here, maybe knows you've inherited?"

She swallowed down a sudden bad taste in her mouth. "Luke. Luke Sullivan. He's my ex-boyfriend, and he was here just yesterday. Or the day before." She honestly couldn't remember. The days seemed to all roll into one suddenly. "I can't believe he'd sneak into the house, but...."

"But he knows you're here, and he's not in your current situation," the cop finished for her, nodding. "We'll check him out. Any idea where he's staying?"

"No. I think he said, but I was too upset at the time to pay attention. I'm sorry."

"That's alright, ma'am. We'll find him and see if he's on the up and up."

She nodded. "Thank you, officer."

"Jenkins, ma'am. Todd Jenkins. If you have any more problems, don't hesitate to ask for me by name, alright?"

She forced herself fully into the present and managed a little smile. "Thank you, Officer Jenkins. I'll do that."

He tipped his fingers to his hat, then strode across her porch and down the steps. The little cluster of cop cars started to break up and pull off down the driveway. Soon, she was alone.

God, she was so glad her mother was coming over for the weekend—

The diaries. She couldn't let Mom see the diaries.

Or... should she? Maybe? Good grief, should she have shown the cops? These were apparently unsolved murders, after all. Should she have handed over the entire trunk and let them go to town closing cases left and right?

Part of her recoiled from doing that. GeeGee had been a pillar of the community. A help to those in need, be that spiritual or physical need. Yes, people had called her a witch under their breaths, but they'd been happy to buy specialized lotions and salves from her to fix acne or solve that back pain or wipe out that embarrassing rash they don't want to talk to their doctor about.

Delia didn't want to ruin that. Didn't want to sully an otherwise sterling reputation.

Did she?

Wracked with an entirely new string of questions for which she had no answer, Delia went back inside, then just stood on the mat, thinking. GeeGee. An intruder in her room. The diaries. Mom coming the day after tomorrow.

She felt sick. Genuinely sick. Her stomach lurched, and she hurried toward GeeGee's bathroom, if only because it was the closest. She knelt in front of the toilet, her stomach roiling and her throat clenching, but nothing came up. She didn't vomit. Not yet, anyway.

"GeeGee, what am I supposed to do?"

She closed her eyes and listened, but there was no answer. If spirits really were real, GeeGee's must have passed through the Veil already. She wondered again if… maybe a séance…?

No. She still didn't believe in ghosts, and she didn't need GeeGee's advice on what to do about her murderous adventures. For right now, she would do nothing. She'd read more, try to figure out how GeeGee did it and got away with it, and then she'd decide what to do.

Tell the police, she figured. Eventually, she'd have to tell the police. She'd have to hand over the diaries and let the cops deal with the fallout. She didn't want to ruin GeeGee's reputation, but if that reputation was all a lie, maybe it should be ruined.

Sick again, she waited to vomit but didn't quite manage it. Sighing, she got up off the floor and went to the sink to wash her hands and rinse her mouth out anyway. Then, she stared at herself in the mirror and wondered how her life had changed so much in such a short time. A month ago, she'd been minding her business, miserable but scratching out a life, in California.

Then, GeeGee had died. That had made all the difference in so many ways.

Shaking off the problem by turning away from the mirror, she went into the bedroom and looked at the diary on the bed. She shouldn't have just left it there, she supposed. Any one of the cops poking around the house could've picked it up and read it and gotten the thrill of a lifetime, but they hadn't. Miraculously.

She supposed there was nothing to be done this morning, except maybe to make some phone calls so Julie and Mom would know what was happening. Not the diaries, of course, but the intruder. That was surely more important than some old diaries filled with macabre fairy tales.

Or maybe part of her still hoped it couldn't be true. That GeeGee—sweet, funny, kind GeeGee—couldn't be a vile serial killer struggling to define herself in print form.

If she just knew how... or maybe where... she could... maybe research? See if there were deaths to match up to what GeeGee claimed as a kill? Would she have been brazen enough to write about her actual crimes in the diary instead of just admitting to them *en masse*?

She needed to read more, she decided. She needed a break—some morning gardening sounded refreshingly normal, as did some breakfast—and then she could read all afternoon, if she wanted. And she did want, she realized, turning back around on the mat to go back outside. She did want to read more. She needed to *know*.

As she went to the shed for her tools and another basket, Delia wondered if that need to know would be the death of her.

20

I never went to medical school, but a dear friend of mine did, and he told me the most amazing thing that changed my life forever. I'd already killed three men by then, but I was so, so lucky. I wasn't even suspected, let alone caught. I hadn't learned my skill set yet, you see. I was still so very green.

But this medical school friend—who shall remain nameless, as I could never implicate him in my own crimes. None of this was his fault—told me that if you inject someone with air, it will almost inevitably kill them. It must be in a vein, of course, not the muscle. It's especially foolproof if you can somehow inject directly into the central nervous system. It's called an air embolism, and it is shockingly quick.

The wealth of possibilities that fact opened up to me was astonishing. My prior kills had been so sloppy. Men who intended me harm and paid for it with their lives. But those deaths were... unsatisfying. Necessary. And difficult to clean up after, if I'm honest. The possibility of a manner of death that didn't require a clean-up was, frankly, quite welcome.

It took some practice, but I became quite adept at delivering an injection into a vein very quickly and accurately. On my fifth attempt, I got it exactly right the first shot and never looked back. Oh,

I sometimes made a flub of it, but only if I was in public and couldn't get a good angle on my mark.

Perhaps I should've been a nurse.

Delia shuddered and closed the diary on her finger, turning away to reach for her cup of tea. She almost regretted eating breakfast now. That last line alone gave her active shivers up and down her spine. She'd heard of medical professionals becoming Angels of Death, as it were, injecting all sorts of poisonous concoctions into people's IV lines at hospitals to "put them out of their misery", even if they weren't in misery to begin with.

Thank god GeeGee hadn't gone into the medical field. How many could she have killed when they were at their most vulnerable?

On my fifth attempt. What had happened to those five? What had happened to the first three? Who had they been? How did they die? What did the clean-up require?

Did she really want to know?

The hot tea soothed her a little, and she was able to reopen the book and start again on the next entry. It was dated only a few days after that last zinger.

I suppose I jumped too far ahead. I don't quite know how to tell this story, even to myself. Goddess, I hope no one ever reads this journal. I'm not fit for prison. I don't take orders well, and I will defend myself to the death, if necessary. That wouldn't go over well in a prison environment, I don't think. Plus, it would be quite unpleasant.

My first, as it were, was in high school. You know how high school boys are. The slightest wind makes their little winkie tinks stand up and demand attention, and they think they are owed that attention. And we women have no say in the matter.

Well, I had a say in the matter. I didn't mean to, but he's the one who brought a pocket knife, so perhaps he deserved to be castrated and bleed out on his own picnic blanket. That was a horrifically difficult scene to clean up, but once I found a place to hide him, he stayed hidden. Everyone thought he'd run away to California.

He always wanted to be a movie star. Well, thanks to me, everyone thought he left to be one.

Now that my little nest egg is starting to grow, perhaps I'll buy that land. Make it my own. Make it so no one will ever stumble across that rolled-up picnic blanket. I've heard of things like that happening. That would be... unfortunate.

AGAIN, DELIA CLOSED THE BOOK ON HER FINGER AND REACHED for her teacup, this time with a shaking hand. She had the most awful, bloody vision in her brain, and she wanted to wash it out somehow.

Sadly, the tea didn't do the job. The image of a high school boy bleeding out through his severed penis did not leave her brain.

Unsatisfying, GeeGee had said of her first three kills. Not messy. Not distressing. *Unsatisfying.*

Horrified, Delia stared off into her great grandaunt's pleasant, cozy room and tried not to think of all that blood. She wasn't ready for such a scene. She hadn't considered....

But she should have expected it. Death at the hands of another wasn't something that could be pretty, no matter how pleasing the prose. Perhaps that very pleasantness of tone was what made it all so horrifying. It was... matter of fact. Stated as if it were the obvious conclusion to a high school boy's advances.

Or perhaps they'd been more than advances? Maybe the boy had been trying to rape her. Did that make it okay? But wouldn't GeeGee have said as much if that was the cause of her actions?

Confused and sick and wishing she'd never started this whole nightmare dip into GeeGee's prior life, Delia looked down at the book in her hands and dreaded what was to come. Because she couldn't stop reading now. She had to know.

She was curious. God help her, she was *curious*.

Swallowing down the horror, she put aside her teacup, opened the diary at her finger, and started reading again.

> But it's been perhaps twenty years since then, and no one has found him, so I should be safe. No one even looked for him. He was that sort.
>
> My second... oh, dear. That was also high school. A football player who thought me being a cheerleader meant he could have at me any time he wanted. He wasn't quite as messy, but only because I'd started carrying my own pocket knife after my first, and I had a better idea where to stick it.
>
> Ha. Men apparently aren't the only ones who dream of where to poke people.

DESPITE HERSELF, DELIA FOUND HERSELF NODDING GRIMLY. SHE didn't want to agree with GeeGee right now, but... men could be like that. Luke had been. So had the three other men she'd dated seriously. And the one guy in college who'd damn near raped her before her roommate walked in and caught him in the act.

Lordy, that had been a scene, but in the end, the guy suffered no consequences. It was "he said, she said", even though there were two she saids. Appalling. And instructive.

But she did not want to think about that son of a bitch while reading about GeeGee's kills. Gritting her teeth, she returned her attention to the page.

> *The third one... well, I suppose you could say I led him to it, but only in the sense that I picked the spot. I knew he would try if he could just get me alone, and I was right. This was my first year of college, and I still carried a pocket knife everywhere I went, either in my pocket or in my purse.*
>
> *They never found the body. They never found any of the three bodies. Perhaps it was the time—this was the late sixties, and plenty of college-age boys were only at college to dodge the draft. The assumption was either that they'd quit and been drafted, or that they'd gone north to try for Canada. I know for a fact that everyone assumed Everett had gone to Canada.*
>
> *And then I met my medical school friend, and all of that messiness vanished in a flash. Suddenly, I didn't even have to hide the body if I didn't want to.*
>
> *I did start carrying a purse more often, though. So few pockets are large enough to hide a syringe.*
>
> *But that is another subject, though one upon which I have a very loud opinion. Perhaps, when my current business venture has run its course, I'll start a clothing line and give all the dresses and trousers huge pockets.*

DELIA GRINNED DESPITE HERSELF. THAT WAS GEEGEE RIGHT down to the ground. In all the time Delia had known the woman, she'd been loud in her protests about women's fashion not making room for the practicality of pocket space.

For a moment, she almost forgot she was reading the confessions of a serial murderer.

The next line reminded her harshly.

As I said, it took me five tries to get the air embolism in the right place on the first try, but I did manage eventually. I won't go into detail about those five less than perfect attempts. All I can say is that they weren't bloody, and they were deserved. Men are pigs, as Somerset Maugham said in <u>Rain</u>. Filthy, dirty pigs.

The first time I got it right on the first try, though... I knew. I knew that it was right. This was what I'd been seeking my whole life. It was clear, crystalline, and pure, that feeling. It shot right through me and told me that, for the first time in my life, all was well within me.

I loved that feeling. I still love it. Sex has never been so clean and pure.

AT THAT LAST LINE OF THE ENTRY, DELIA FELT HORRIBLY SAD. She couldn't explain why. Perhaps because it sounded like GeeGee had never felt right when she wasn't killing, and that was inexpressibly awful.

She again closed the book on her finger, reaching for her tea. It was one of GeeGee's special herbal blends. For soothing calmness, which Delia had assumed she would need with her reading task. She'd been right, though it was a contradictory sort of calmness. How could the same woman who'd committed such cold, calculated murders make such lovely, calming tea? Blend such soothing fragrances?

She would never understand, and that was perhaps for the best. She didn't think she wanted to understand GeeGee's reasonings. She didn't want to think like a serial killer.

Unsettled, she put aside both the tea and the diary and

decided abruptly to do something, literally anything else for a while. Anything would do.

Wiping her hands together as if she'd touched something vile and was trying to rub them clean, Delia left the room at a near-run.

21

GeeGee retired from all her business flights at the age of fifty-eight, and her investments had kept making money since then. Delia looked up from the financial reports Barrett had emailed her with a wonder that bordered on fear. Did she dare attempt to build on that success, or should she just coast on the interest of all that capital, not risking what GeeGee had so painstakingly raised?

Her phone chimed, and she picked it up, recognizing the number from talking to Barrett before.

"Mr. Davidson?"

"Just Barrett, Miss Delia." He sounded as if he was smiling. "Did you get the email?"

She huffed. "I did, but I don't know if I really understand it. How on earth did GeeGee manage all of this?"

"With a lot of help." Now, he sounded amused. "Please don't feel like you have to take a crash course on Miss Virginia's investment portfolio. I will always answer any questions you have and will gladly talk about her strategies any time you choose, but if you don't want to go that same route, the current investment strategy can continue uninterrupted for years." Less amused, he continued. "Of course, the current run of the market is concerning, but not to your net worth. Miss Virginia lessened her investment portfolio in the past several years, perhaps sensing the coming softness in the market, so there isn't a chance of any significant loss."

Delia shook her head. "I guess I'm glad for that. I didn't even know the market was soft. Or even really what that means. I am so not cut out for this."

"Not to worry, Miss Delia. That's what we're here for. I just wanted you to have a snapshot of Miss Virginia's current financial picture and the likely implications of your inheritance. Frankly, I wanted you to know that you never have to worry about money again, even if you make no changes at all to the current strategy. Miss Virginia did very well before she retired, and she's done perfectly well since then. And so will you."

That, at least, was a relief.

"Good. Thank you for that, Barrett. I really do appreciate you explaining. I was doing good to make rent before this. I just don't have the vocabulary for success."

He chuckled politely. "It won't take you very long to pick it up if your great grandaunt was right about you. She always said you had twice the intellect you credited yourself with, and she was always so proud of how you graduated tenth in your college class and top of your major."

She winced. A fat lot of good that had done her, finishing top of her computer science class. She'd thought working for a major internet company in California would be so much better than working somewhere in Missouri, but she'd been so, so wrong. Miserably wrong.

But now, none of that mattered. She could do whatever she wanted, even if that was just read GeeGee's creepy diaries and play video games all day.

"Well, she had high hopes," she finally said, feeling uncomfortable with the thought that GeeGee had been so proud of her. "But I don't know if I'll ever understand finance. I think I'll take your advice and leave most of that to your... group. Your people."

"That will be fine, as well," Barrett assured her. "You won't be disappointed."

"Okay." But that felt inadequate. "Thank you."

Nope. Still inadequate. Thankfully, he rolled on with the conversation without seeming to need anything more from her.

"No problem, Miss Delia. We'll talk soon. And remember, if you need more funds, I'm sure we can work that out. Please don't worry about anything. I'm sure that's not what your great grandaunt would want for you."

The worst part was... that was true. GeeGee would've never wanted Delia to worry. Just like she never would've wanted Delia to read her diaries. Would that she could turn back time and never discover the damn things.

But she was in it now, and she supposed she'd have to read them all. But not right now. Right now, she still wanted to do literally anything else.

A truck, she decided. She wanted to buy a farm truck so she could get around.

Inspired, she pulled out her phone and scrolled the ride share program, hoping she could request Patricia. She didn't feel like dealing with another stranger after talking to the police this morning. She wanted a friendly face.

Thankfully, Patricia was available, and Delia had her Uber set up in no time. Now, she just had to burn a quick fifteen minutes for the colorful driver to get here. What should she do for such a short period of time?

An idea flashed in her mind, but she hesitated to act on it. She suddenly wanted to know... no. She didn't. She wouldn't go look at the last diary in the trunk to see if GeeGee was still a serial killer at eighty-some-odd years of age.

And yet, her feet took her that direction without input from her conscious will. Before she could talk herself out of it, she stood before the closet with the door open, looking down at the trunk. She should've pulled the dresses back into place to cover it, what with all the police running around this morning, but she'd been too upset about the break-in—the walk-in, she reminded herself, vowing to lock the door whether she was home or not from now on—to do so.

Biting at her lower lip, she leaned down, opened the trunk, and picked up what she assumed was the most recent volume. It was the closest to the bottom right-hand corner and was the only one leaning against the others. Surely, it was the most recent.

Steeling herself, she opened it and flipped to the last entry, which was, distressingly, from the weekend just before she passed. It wasn't a very long entry. Delia couldn't begin to guess if that was good or bad.

All my spirit guides tell me that my time is coming, and soon. Everything goes to Delia, of course. She deserves it, and she needs it more than all the other relatives. Vultures, the lot of them. They've been waiting for me to die for years, but not Delia. Goddess, I've missed her.

You know, I rather hope she finds these diaries some day. I won't show them to her myself, but if she happens across them... well, I hope she won't think too badly of me. I've tried to be good enough to outweigh the bad, but the fact is that I just don't feel very bad about the bad. I never have. Those men deserved what they got.

And I have a distressing feeling that Delia's ex young man deserves what he would get if I were even a decade younger, but I would never do that to my dear girl. She doesn't deserve the heartache his death would inevitably cost her, even though they're through. The poor girl. She so deserves love, and his kind is simply incapable of it.

There were times I wished she would grow up to be a lesbian, just so she wouldn't have to give her fragile, tender heart to a man. I was never so lucky, and I don't think she is, either. Bless her.

Anyway, if she does read these diaries... Delia, my love, child of my heart, forgive me. I won't apologize for being good at being bad, but I do apologize for any upset these pages cause you. My only request is that you read them all if you read any of them. Don't judge me on my skill set.

I did what I thought was best. That's all I've ever done, dear girl.

I love you.

GRIEF AND HORROR MIXED INSIDE HER, AND DELIA WISHED SHE hadn't skipped ahead, though it appeared GeeGee had known she'd do exactly that. GeeGee knew her better than anyone. Then again, Delia thought she knew her great grandaunt better than anyone, too.

Maybe they hadn't really known each other at all. Forgive her? Was that even a possibility?

Delia frankly hadn't thought that far ahead.

Shaking her head, she leaned the book back into place against the prior volume, pulled the dresses toward the center and spaced them out evenly, then closed the closet doors. She didn't know what to do. Hell, she probably should have told the cops about the literal trunk full of incriminating evidence in the closet this morning, but she hadn't been thinking about that.

Or was that not the full truth? Had she been deliberately *not* thinking about the diaries while the police were here? Had she been, perhaps, covering for GeeGee? She knew she didn't want to destroy the woman's reputation, but she surely hadn't decided against saying something entirely... had she?

A horn blipped jauntily outside, and she jumped, stirring to action. She'd spent much longer in thought than she'd expected, and now she didn't have time to change out of the cardigan and into a flannel shirt like she'd planned. Oh, well. It was one of GeeGee's cardigans and had that overwhelming scent of patchouli about it, but it would have to do. She didn't have time to change.

She did, however, grab both her old keys and the new ones, finagling them onto the ring as she headed for the door and remembering to lock said door behind her. It felt as strange as everything else about her move back to Missouri. She felt… out of step. As if not a single thing she'd considered solid rock was actually solid.

Forcing a smile she didn't feel, she waved back at Patricia's enthusiastic gesturing, then climbed into the back seat, preparing herself for an afternoon full of people-ing. Good god.

"There she is," Patricia said, smiling back over the seat at her. "More shopping? Decided to do a *Pretty Woman*, after all?"

"Car shopping," she said, trying to sound like a normal. "Truck shopping, actually. I need a good, solid farm truck that doesn't cost a fortune." She pulled out the business card she'd stuffed into her pocket this morning and handed it over the seat. "Do you know the place?"

"I do." She looked disappointed, though. "No Cooper? I thought we were friends."

That earned a surprised chuckle. "Sorry, but I'm a practical sort of girl."

"No fun." But Patricia grinned and turned back toward the front and put the car in gear. "But I guess the customer is always right."

Delia snorted. "The customer, in my experience, is an idiot. And I say that as a customer."

Patricia shot her a green-eyed glance in the mirror, her eyes crinkled at the corners. "I won't argue with that, although I probably should."

"Don't." She almost snorted again but didn't want to come

across as bitter. "I worked at an IT Help Desk for five years, so I'm probably not the best judge, but I still think it's true."

"Wow, IT, huh?" Another glance from those sparkling green eyes. "So you're really smart?"

She abruptly looked out the window. "I dunno how smart I am. I moved to California and worked for a giant internet company, but I did it for peanuts, so your mileage may vary."

"I don't buy that." Patricia gave a shake of her head without looking away from the road as the town came into being around them, popping up like weeds on the edge of a meadow. "You must be doing something right if you're buying a farm truck for a big property like yours instead of a Cooper for running around all flashy."

She shrugged. "It all depends on the context. You're a driver, so you want a car that speaks to that part of you. I'm now a property owner, so I figured I'd better get something I can drive around the back forty with."

"See? Told ya you were smart." She winked in the rear-view mirror. "It's just up ahead. Do you want me to stick around while you look? I could drive you around the lot so you don't even have to get out if you don't see what you want."

But that wouldn't be necessary. Delia already saw the one she wanted, and they hadn't even pulled into the lot yet. It was an old red truck, the paint faded with years in the sun, a few dents and dings around the fenders signaling a life already spent in the trenches. It looked like anyone's idea of an old farm truck, including the wooden slat sides on the bed.

It was perfect. It was also ridiculously overpriced. Delia didn't need to pull up Kelley Blue Book to know that.

"Nope. I see the one I want." She pointed at it while Patricia negotiated the maze of new vehicles to get back over to the used side of the lot. "There she is. Miss America."

Patricia snorted. "That is so you. I'm not even gonna argue."

Delia broke into a huge grin. "Thanks! Do you mind running

me up to the main building so I can get this show on the road? I'll just drive the truck home, so you don't have to stay."

"If you can even get it started. I can't believe you're buying that old beater, but it's definitely exactly what you said you wanted, so I guess I'll just fall back on the customer always being right." She shot a stern look back at her in the mirror. "Don't you dare pay sticker price, though."

"I won't. I know what she's worth."

"Good."

Patricia hauled the wheel back the other way, doing a U-turn in the middle of the aisle and heading for the main structure in the middle of the lot's maze. There, she put it in park and turned to lean her arm along the back of her seat.

"Not a penny over twelve thousand."

Delia smirked. "They're getting ten-five or nothing."

"Good girl." The red head tilted toward the building. "Go get your truck, Miss Delia."

"Thanks for the ride, Miss Patricia."

Grinning, she opened the door and scooted out of the little car, then waved as Patricia drove off with a jaunty little double honk. Then, she squared her shoulders, straightened her expression, and marched into the cool, spacious sales building. Barrett had suggested she call the bank before making a purchase over ten thousand dollars, assuming—as anyone would—that she'd planned on buying an expensive vehicle to go with her new station in life. She'd balked, but she had indeed called her bank, and it was a good thing, too. They would have declined a purchase of over ten thousand without her prior notification.

Confident with that knowledge in the back of her mind, she strode over to the nearest desk and waited for the lady behind it to look up from the paperwork she was just finishing.

"I'd like to see someone about the old, red farm truck in that first row out front. The Chevy."

One perfectly plucked eyebrow rose. "That old thing? Honey, that's been here since god was a boy. You can do better."

Delia's eyes narrowed. "Does it start?"

"Yeah, but it's a standard."

"I know how to drive a stick. Does it have any holes in the floorboard?"

Those perfect eyebrows drew together. "Uh… no? We wouldn't have a car on our lot that had holes in the floor. Why on earth would you ask that?"

"Because those are my hard lines. If she starts and is sound, I know what I want. The price is ridiculous, though. You'll never get seventeen thousand out of her."

The woman studied her for a moment, then gestured for her to sit down. Delia did so, warily studying her opponent.

"Do you know much about vehicles?"

She shrugged. "Not especially. I just know that's the one I want. I can afford to get it fixed."

"Oh, lord, don't ever say that to a used car salesman."

"Or a saleswoman?"

The women smiled. "I will say that that old thing is almost twenty years old and has over two hundred thousand miles on it."

Delia waved this off. "She'll go another hundred thousand if I take care of her. I'll give you ten thousand five hundred for her right now, or I go elsewhere."

The lady considered for a moment, eyes narrowing, then abruptly shrugged and reached across the desk for a handshake. "Sold. You're right. We were never getting seventeen thousand for it."

Heady with victory, Delia smiled brightly. "Really?"

"Really. Please, call me Vickie."

"I'm Delia. I probably should've led with that. Sorry."

Vickie chuckled. "I could have broken in at any time. I was too surprised by your approach. You looked ready to do battle."

"Did I?" Her cheeks heated. "Sorry. I guess I *was* expecting a fight."

"Honey, I'm not gonna fight over that old truck. She's yours, and well won."

It took a good hour of printing papers, signing, and chatting pleasantly, but by the time Delia walked back out into the early afternoon sunshine, the faded old farm truck was hers. No financing needed. She just needed to pay the sales tax and pick up her tags.

She completely forgot to ask for Mr. Brinkley's nephew.

Vickie stood by as she climbed up into the cab, leaving the door open so she could talk while she fired the old girl up. Her feet practically standing on the clutch and brake, she turned the key in the ignition. The engine wasn't a diesel, but it was almost as loud as one. Delia smiled.

"That's a good sound."

Vickie shook her head. "If you say so. I know enough about trucks to sell them, and that's all I care to know."

Feeling sheepish, Delia shrugged. "I don't even know that much, if I'm honest. But I know what I like, and that's Lola here."

"Lola, huh?"

She nodded, settling her hands on the steering wheel. Someone down the line had wrapped a soft grip around it, so her hands felt easy and comfortable, like they belonged.

"Yup. Lola." She looked down at her sales lady with a grin. "Thank you, Vickie."

"You're very welcome. I hope you like her."

"I do."

Vickie backed up and waved, so Delia reached out and swung the heavy door shut, feeling like a kid perched on the bench seat. She scooched the seat forward, angled all the mirrors, then put her in reverse and eased the clutch out. She hadn't driven a standard in probably a decade, but she figured it was like riding a bike.

So, of course, she killed the engine.

Unperturbed, she patiently went through the procedure again, and this time, she got backed out of the spot and headed in the right direction in no time. She waved again at the sales lady, then got the feel of the steering wheel and the pull of the tires as she wove through the lot a couple of times before getting out into traffic.

When she felt secure enough with exactly how much play the clutch had, she pulled onto the main drag and joined the flow. It had been three years since she drove herself anywhere, and it felt freeing. Even all the watchfulness, the paying attention, felt like a release. She could go anywhere she wanted now.

A glance at the gas gauge told her that she could go anywhere she wanted on less than an eighth of a tank of gas. Grinning, she found the nearest gas station and pulled in to fill ol' Lola up.

Patricia was right. Gas was stupidly expensive.

Then, she was on her way home, the breeze in her hair as she rolled down the window to prop her elbow on the edge like an old farmer.

Free at last, as the old song said. Delia liked the sound of that.

For a little while, she was free.

22

After checking the locks at least three times and eating an early supper, Delia brewed up a pot of jasmine green tea with a dab of honey, then took the pot and a cup into GeeGee's bedroom to read in the wingback. The heady freedom from earlier was gone. She may be home, but home came with new responsibilities she could never have dreamed of.

GeeGee didn't pull any punches, either. The next entry started off with a punch right to the gut.

> *I hate to have anything in common with as truly demented a person as John Wayne Gacy, but I did learn a valuable lesson from his atrocities.*
>
> *Don't shit where you eat.*

DELIA NEARLY CHOKED ON HER TEA.

I didn't know that from the start, of course. Gacy had only just started when I already had several kills under my belt. But I learned from his sort, from what I saw on the news about killers who got caught, who tripped up and landed themselves in jail. I learned from their mistakes.

While those news reports weren't always about serial killers, I'm sure some of them were. We're not new at all. I've found histories of folk who killed folk in a series going back hundreds of years. It's possible that the Beast of Gévaudan was actually just an overly hairy serial killer protected by a high politician family member, and that was more than three hundred years ago.

I am disappointed to learn, however, that most of my kind in my own sex reap their own children. I've never had any children and don't plan to, but I could never take one of my nephews or my niece. I can't imagine harming someone so helpless.

Where would be the challenge in that?

DISMAYED, DELIA REALIZED THAT SHE HAD, AGAIN, BEEN ON THE verge of agreeing with, even sympathizing with GeeGee, only to have her say something so cold and callous that it took her breath away. If only GeeGee weren't such an engaging autobiographer. It was impossible to not be invested.

Gritting her teeth, she read on.

But there are ladies more like me who kill because they must. Jane Toppan, a nurse who killed at least two dozen of her patients at the turn of the twentieth century. I read that she got a sexual satisfaction out of it that I don't feel, but she also said that she wanted to kill more people than anyone else in the world. I can relate to that, although her patients were, by and large, helpless.

That holds no thrill for me. It's the challenge that sings through me at the moment of victory.

More in my line is the imminently more practical Anna Marie Hahn, a German gambler who poisoned old men for their money in the '30s. However, she killed people she had befriended, had been seen with, and thus, her downfall. She was immediately suspected when her method was revealed on autopsy, and she went to the electric chair. Nasty way to go.

I can respect her, though. She punched up, as it were.

Tillie Klimek, though she also was quickly suspected due to killing those she knew, was an enterprising woman that I also respect. It was said that she could predict someone's death, only to have confessed to their murders later. She also killed her husbands for profit, which pleases me greatly.

There are so many more in this country alone and, I suspect, around the world. I am not alone, although I feel that I will fare better than my gruesome peers because I no longer take those I know. I learned from my forebears.

Don't shit where you eat.

DELIA REACHED FOR HER TEA, SHAKING HER HEAD, THEN TURNED the page to the next entry. She'd always known GeeGee was a brilliant woman with a cut-throat business sense who had succeeded at everything she'd tried, but she'd had no idea how terrifying that sort of ruthless intelligence could be.

It was also distressing how GeeGee referred to other serial killers as her "kind", as if they were a separate but compatible species of human. What had she said back in that first entry? She was a different sort of human, but she was still a human?

Nauseating. But fascinating.

Troubled, both by the neat writing and her own reaction to it, Delia went back to her reading.

. . .

My brother was married today. I played the part, but this is his second marriage, and I have no doubt it will end as the first one did—in heartache and tears. I don't understand why people don't just remain alone. It's so much better to be alone than to have to hide who you are just to stay.

I also made my first million this week. I don't feel settled yet, as I read once that the difference between the rich and the truly wealthy is that the rich may have a bolus of money and then spend and spend until they go broke, but the truly wealthy never spend what they earn. They invest and diversify to the point that they make more money by simply continuing to breathe.

I will be truly wealthy. I will have what I was told was not for me. And I will do it on my own. A partner would only hinder my ascension by taking what I've earned for himself. I have no doubt I would eventually kill him in his sleep and end like so many women before me —executed for freeing themselves.

Anyway, I also learned a new trick, perhaps spurred on by my talk of Tillie Klimek the other day. I've learned to read tarot cards. I met a marvelous woman at a county fair who clearly had no psychic ability whatsoever or she would have run screaming from her tent when she read my palm.

But she did intrigue me, and we had a lovely chat about how much of tarot reading was natural psychic ability and how much was the learned trick of cold reading. I've always had hunches about people, especially men. I've always known which ones would try for me and end up on the tip of my needle and which would treat me with a measure of respect and thus survive, even before they spoke.

Women, though, are harder to read, so I was very interested in this lady's explanation of cold reading. It's shockingly similar to how I make my business decisions—a mix of intuition and a quick reading of the man's (it's always a man in this world of business) facial expressions and answers to key, leading questions.

I will practice this skill until intuition and observation merge into one intimidating talent. I want people—men—to fear me, at least a little. I want them to wonder what I know and how I know it, and I want to read their secrets right out of their eyes, steal them from their over-aggressive handshakes.

I will be wealthy, and I will do it by walking my sensible business pumps right up their bent backs.

DELIA SIPPED HER TEA, AGAIN MOVED TO BOTH ADMIRATION AND fear of GeeGee and unsure how to feel about it.

As she settled the cup into the niche in the saucer and began to read the next entry, the doorbell sounded. Irritation flared through her, as it had when her mother had called her to dinner while she was in the middle of a good book as a teenager. Grinning ruefully at the thought that all this serial killer talk made for such good reading, she carefully placed the book, current spot opened and face-down, under GeeGee's pillow. No more leaving it in plain sight on the bedspread.

Satisfied and wondering if it was still considered harboring a murderer if said murderer was already dead, Delia left the room and went into the foyer, pausing at the tall outline of shadow outside the door on her porch. Luke again? Or maybe the cop from this morning?

Fidgeting, she debated pretending she wasn't home, but then the doorbell rang again and she shook herself. If it was Luke, she'd slam the door in his face. If it was the cop, she'd invite him in, secure in the knowledge that he surely wouldn't go looking under GeeGee's pillow for a full-sized intruder.

Squaring her shoulders, Delia opened the door.

23

"Elijah?"

She couldn't be more surprised if GeeGee stood on the porch. What on earth...?

But her old friend grinned crookedly and scruffed at his hair in an old gesture that raised a thousand echoes.

"Most people just call me Eli now. Sounds less Old Testament, don't you think?"

She blinked, mouth hanging open with shock. He shifted his feet and tried again.

"I heard you had some trouble this morning and was worried. Are you okay?"

A dim bell rang far in the back of her mind. An alarm bell, or a wake-up bell? Honestly, it could go either way at the moment.

She shook her head, trying to gather her thoughts.

"Heard how?"

He grinned crookedly again. "Small town. Everyone knows everything."

Her eyes narrowed, her thoughts picking back up, and he chuckled.

"Okay, okay. I have a police band radio in my office. When I heard your address, I knew I had to come check to make sure you were okay for myself. I'd have never gotten to sleep tonight, otherwise."

Eyes still narrow, she deliberately leaned out to look up at the darkened sky, as if the dusk-to-dawn porch light being on didn't tell the story by simply being on.

"I just got off work. Look, Delia, I'm trying to be your old friend here." His head tilted to one side. "Whatever it was really got you nervous, didn't it? That's fair, you know. What actually happened?"

An ancient urge to invite him in assailed her, but she shoved it away with effort. The last thing she wanted was sit-down company, and not just because she was reading GeeGee's murder diaries in her dead great grandaunt's room.

"Intruder," she finally said, not intending to sound short but unable to help herself. "Someone broke in while I was in another room. Snuck up the stairs and escaped out my bedroom window."

She cringed internally at admitting that she was staying in her old bedroom, but she didn't really think Elijah—Eli, she reminded herself—was the intruder. Did she?

"Jesus, no wonder you're so jumpy." He shook his head. "What a welcome back home, huh?"

She huffed reluctantly. "You could say that." She put a hand on the doorknob and took a step back. "Look, thank you for stopping by, but I'm kind of in the middle of something—"

"Oh, sorry." He put up both hands. "I didn't even think about that, but I did just drop by without notice." The crooked grin came back. "Of course, I would've called if I had your number."

It was a hint, and not a subtle one. She debated, then wondered if she'd be this reluctant if she weren't reading GeeGee's cultured ravings. Sighing, she gave in.

"Get your phone out."

He hurried to do so, almost dropping it as he pulled it from the inner pocket of his business suit jacket. "Okay, go."

She said the numbers quickly, almost hoping he wouldn't get them all.

He nodded, thumbs tapping rapidly. "Got it. Thanks, Delia. I'll text you some warning next time."

She couldn't help it. She rolled her eyes. Leave it to a man to assume she'd want him to stop by again.

But that was GeeGee talking. Delia was... a little relieved. It made her feel less alone to know someone she knew and used to trust was right here in town if something else went wrong.

That didn't mean she wanted him waltzing in and out any old time, though.

"I should get going. You're probably just sitting down to dinner."

Was he angling for an invitation? Too bad.

"I already ate, but like I said, I am in the middle of something, so...."

"Message received." But he grinned again, unconcerned, as he backed away across the porch. "It's good to have you home, Delia."

The old urge to relate to her friend had her answering before she could rethink it. "It's good to be home, Elij—uh, Eli."

He nodded, grinned softly, then turned and trotted down the steps, the tail of his suit jacket flapping as he went. It was oddly boyish behavior for someone in that sharp a suit, but she only shook her head and shut the door instead of watching him all the way to his car. She did, however, stand by the door until she heard said car start and drive away before going back to GeeGee's bedroom.

The last thing she wanted was further interruption.

Carefully removing the diary from under the pillow without bending any pages, she settled into the wingback and looked down at the next entry. Girding her loins, she began to read.

24

The floor creaked downstairs.

Delia sat up in bed, startled awake at the sharp crack of sound, a shout pushing at her throat. She swallowed it back and reached for her phone on the nightstand next to the bed, pausing to listen before hitting the emergency 911 button.

Nothing. Absolute silence. No breeze outside. No creaks of shifting weight on hardwoods. Just her heart beating madly in her throat and her breath, light and quick in the semi-dark.

Nothing. Just the house shifting. Must have been.

But she stayed sitting up in bed for a long while, wondering how long it would take to wait out whoever might be frozen mid-step downstairs, waiting for it to be okay to move again. A less sharp creak finally slithered into the silence, as if someone was very carefully shifting their weight. Her breath caught in her throat.

Suddenly, the chimes on the back patio clanged loudly, as if someone had run face-first into them, and she jumped out of bed, her phone in her hand, and ran to the door, already calling 911.

"911, what's the address of the emergency?"

"The Hollows, out on old 66. There's someone in my house, and there's someone out on the back patio, too. Hurry!"

She didn't stay on the line. Instead, she shoved the phone into the pocket of her pajama pants and ran down the steps to the kitchen, going again for a knife only to stop and stare out the bank of windows into the dark. The wind chimes hung still and silent. Shouldn't they be swinging if they'd been run into?

Shaking off that thought, she grabbed the big knife and started turning on all the lights in the lower floor. She knew no one had fled up the stairs, or she'd have met them in the hall. How the hell had they gotten in? She'd locked the front and back doors—

The windows. She hadn't locked the windows, and as she flicked on the light in the parlor, she realized that, though all the windows were closed, one of them was missing a screen. Jesus, someone really had been in the house.

A few moments later, she was sure no one was hiding in any closets—she'd neatly tucked GeeGee's 1981 diary back in the trunk and covered it with dresses—as the first cop car flew up her driveway, gravel flying and lights strobing in the dark. No siren in due deference to the hour, but a definite sense of urgency. Delia appreciated that.

She appreciated even more that it was Officer Jenkins climbing out of his cruiser with his hand on his gun.

"Are you all right, Miss Jameson?"

"Yes, thank you, Officer Jenkins, but someone was downstairs maybe fifteen minutes ago. They got in through the parlor window. It's the only place low enough to climb in without a step ladder, and I forgot to lock the windows. I'm sorry."

"Not your fault." He gestured toward the windows in question. "The one without the screen?"

She nodded and climbed down the steps, wrapped up in one of GeeGee's cardigans again with shoes on her feet. She'd gone back upstairs for them when she realized she was truly alone in the house, then had needed the comfort of a cardigan, even if it was GeeGee's. Maybe especially because it was GeeGee's.

Old habits were hard to break.

"It's on the ground. They must not have had time to put it back in on the way out."

He nodded, then looked back at the next police cruiser rolling up the driveway, strobes flashing.

"I'll have Gibbons take it in for fingerprinting, just in case. He'd be dumb not to wear gloves, but you never know. The world is full of dumb criminals."

She smiled a little, though her face still felt numb. "Makes your job easier?"

"You'd think." Officer Jenkins quit shining his light around the house and property and finally looked directly at her. "The dispatcher said someone was out on the back deck, too?"

"Patio. Yeah, this way. It sounded like someone ran into the wind chimes, but—"

She cut herself off. He looked at her strangely as she hesitated to lead the way.

"But what?"

"Nothing. I'm sure it was nothing. It's this way."

She led the way around to the back of the house and pointed at the wind chimes, hanging still and silent in the cool, calm night. Had they really been that still just after that big jangle?

What did it mean if they were?

Officer Jenkins, on the other hand, was shining his light on the ground underneath them, frowning as he shone it this way and that.

"I don't see any footprints in the grass."

"Hm?"

"No crushed grass. It doesn't look to me like anyone was back here."

Unease crawled up her spine. What did it mean?

"Maybe they were standing on the patio itself? Not the grass?"

"Maybe." He didn't sound convinced, though, shining the flashlight all around the periphery of the patio tiles. "Doesn't look like anyone was walking anywhere around here."

Maybe it was my imagination, she almost said, then bit her tongue. The last thing she wanted this cop thinking was that she was a hysterical female calling 911 willy-nilly. She'd never get another officer out here again if he thought that.

His walkie squawked, and he pulled it off his belt to mutter into it. She looked at the uncrushed grass around the patio, then up at the silent wind chimes. Did it mean anything? Were there two people out for her, or…?

She didn't let herself think what could've happened if the wind chimes hadn't clanged exactly when they did.

"Miss Jameson?"

She blinked off her thoughts and looked at him. "Yes?"

"Gibbons is already on her way back to town with your screen. We'll run a few tests on it to see if we can come up with something. We can assign someone to park in your driveway the rest of the night—"

"Oh, surely that's not necessary?"

He shrugged. "I honestly don't know. I just know that you've been broken in on twice in twenty-four hours, and that doesn't bode well. Our response time is great inside the city limits, but out here in the boonies, it's a different story. I don't like the idea of you out here alone with no help for seven and a half minutes."

She hesitated. "I don't suppose you were able to find Luke?"

"No, unfortunately. Did you remember where he said he'd be?"

Sighing, she shook her head. "I think he just said he'd be around, but I'm not sure. I'm sorry."

"Can you give us a description?" He whipped out a notebook

and pen. "If he's breaking into your house, he may be staying under an assumed name."

"Uh… five foot ten? Black hair and blue eyes. Pale skin. Athletic build. He plays a lot of basketball. Um…." She thought back, reluctantly trying to picture more than just the basic look of him. "He has a Razorback tattoo on his left—no, right bicep. Big Razorbacks fan."

"Great." He jotted furiously in his notebook. "That'll get us started. Has he ever gone by any other names that you know of?"

"No."

"Okay. I mean it about having someone stay in the driveway overnight. It's only for a few more hours, anyway."

She hedged, then reluctantly nodded. "I'd appreciate that, Officer Jenkins. I don't know that I'll be able to sleep, but at least I won't be climbing the walls."

He huffed and flipped his notebook closed, tucking it into his belt. "I'd say don't worry, but you have good reason to do so. But someone will be just out of sight around the first turn if anything else happens. I'll make sure he calls you before leaving in the morning, too. We have your number."

"Thank you, Officer Jenkins."

He nodded. "No problem. Try to get some sleep."

She smiled faintly. That probably wouldn't happen, but she saw no need to burst his bubble.

He left with a tip of his fingers to his trooper hat. She stayed looking up at the wind chimes for a moment, then followed him around just in time to see him get into his cruiser. She waved as he backed up and turned around. She couldn't tell in the dark if he waved back.

Then, just like that, she was alone. Well, alone as far as the first turn in the driveway.

Sighing, she climbed back up to the porch and went over to sit in the porch swing. It was late enough in the season and cool enough that no bugs swarmed around the porch light, so she just sat in the swing for a long moment before beginning to swing gently. She didn't go enough for the chains to creak, just enough to not be completely still.

Someone had broken in. Twice. Who could it be? It had to be Luke, right?

The image of a crooked grin broke through her thoughts, and she abruptly stopped swinging. Elijah knew she was in town. He'd been on this very porch just this evening. He seen her at that store even before Luke showed up. Surely, he wouldn't...?

Huddling in GeeGee's cardigan, she wondered when her life had become so fraught. Just a day ago, she'd been getting used to the thought of being rich, living footloose and fancy free. Yes, she was still grieving, but that was one cloud on an otherwise bright blue sky.

Now, though, GeeGee was a serial killer, and someone was breaking into her house, not for valuables but for *her*.

Jesus. She hadn't even been here for a week.

Frowning, she stood out of the swing and went back inside to methodically lock all the windows on the ground floor. Then, because that didn't feel like enough, she went around the second floor and locked all of those, too. She checked her bedroom windows twice, just to be sure. Then, she went downstairs, made a pot of tea, and headed for the old wingback.

If she couldn't sleep, she might as well read. It had served her well enough in her youth. It should serve her well enough now.

Even if she was reading about murder.

25

The best place to strike, which also works the fastest, is in the back of the neck just below the base of the skull, shooting the air directly into the brain. An air embolism there works in moments. It has never failed me.

It's not always the easiest place to get to, however, so I have found a few other places that work, though not as quickly and not as reliably. The femoral vein is quite good for delivering air to the heart quickly, but it can be fiddly to get the injection in just the right spot, and often requires a longer needle than those I carry with me. Not recommended unless you have the time to strike with precision instead of with rapidity. I have, however, done it exactly right once under a table on a cruise.

Everyone thought he had a stroke. I felt exultant for hours afterward. I never tried that again in public, though. It could have so easily gone wrong and drawn attention. But it was a cruise. So many people die sudden deaths on cruises. If not for that and the probability of food poisoning, I would take so many more cruises.

The axillary vein in the armpit is handy in a pinch, but it's in a mostly inaccessible area unless the man is reaching for you or has his arms up. Not the best for when you don't want to draw attention, but *excellent if you have your prey alone and shirtless, perhaps lying on a hotel bed with his arms tied to the headboard.*

It's strange how often men will allow you to tie them up if they think you will fuck them afterwards. It's also strange how rarely the police think of anything but a sexual encounter turned heart attack when confronted by a dead body tied to a bed in a hotel room.

Directly in the heart is, of course, almost instantly deadly, but the rib cage is an extremely efficient protective device, and you'd again need a longer needle. Again, not good for a quick and deadly encounter and completely useless in public.

Plus, both the heart and the thigh have the possibility of the injection site being seen upon autopsy, where the hair neatly hides a tiny injection mark at the base of the skull or in the armpit. A very thorough medical examiner might find it, but it's unlikely.

The base of the skull is my favorite spot. I often pretend to be wrapping my arms around a man, only to drop him like a sack of pig slop. It also works quite well from behind.

So many men never see me coming. Frankly, no men have ever seen me coming, if you'll pardon the pun.

Delia's eyes burned. The officer who'd spent the night in her driveway had called a good hour ago to inform her that he'd been called back to the station. She thanked him for his time and immediately sank back into GeeGee's dark internal world.

She was into December now, almost finished with this first volume. Her back hurt, her hand was numb from holding onto the book, and she had a headache, but she couldn't stop. Even for breakfast, she couldn't stop reading.

I won't say I've never enjoyed sex, but I've never had an orgasm from a man's fumblings. I've brought myself to ecstasy, but only rarely. I don't seem to need that particular function in life, whereas most of my kind seem to combine it with our need to kill. I don't understand that. The two are quite separate in my mind, other than the ease with which the possibility of sex presents me with victims.

No, I gain far more of a thrill from a perfectly-placed strike than from scratching the itch. That is my desire. That is my bliss. My raison d'être.

That is when I am truly alive.

DELIA'S STOMACH GROWLED AND ROLLED, ALL AT THE SAME TIME. She really should eat something, as she'd eaten early last night and had spent most of the night awake and reading, but she wasn't sure she *could* eat. GeeGee could be uncomfortably graphic when detailing how other serial killers had gotten things wrong and made a mess that eventually got them caught. The woman had done an uncomfortable amount of research, and her stark prose was unrelenting in detail.

Sighing, she stood up out of the wingback and hobbled, her legs asleep from lack of movement, the few steps to the bed to lay it open, face-down, on the bedspread. She really should find some sort of bookmark at some point, if for no other reason than ease of hiding it fast if needed. She shouldn't care about creasing the pages of a murder diary, but she did care.

She stretched, groaning, then touched her stomach when it growled again, more insistently this time. She definitely needed to eat.

Not poached egg and avocado English muffins, though. Maybe never again. She didn't want to ever think about GeeGee while eating.

In the kitchen, she stood at the open refrigerator for a long moment, trying to decide what to make. She needed to hit the grocery store. She could take her new old truck and fill up the bed if she wanted. Smiling a little at the thought, she decided on a fried egg and cheese sandwich.

When she had her breakfast all sorted out, she sat down in the window nook and felt herself grow still again at the sight of the wind chimes. Had they really clanged so harshly last night, just as the intruder started across the floor again? Could they have stopped moving so quickly if they'd rung so loudly moments before?

If not, what did that mean?

And if someone really had been on the patio at the same time as someone was creeping around her ground floor, what did *that* mean? Exactly how many people now had it in for her?

No longer hungry, she looked down at her sandwich and swallowed hard. She needed to eat it. Stress and heartache had already cost her more weight than she cared to lose. She didn't need fear to cost her even more. She didn't want to look like a scarecrow unless it was Halloween.

GeeGee loved Halloween. She always dressed like a witch, of course, but in a different costume every year. She loved scaring the kids—in a healthy, fun way, though, not in a serial killer way—and handing out homemade popcorn balls that even the most paranoid parents would usually let their kids take, so long as GeeGee promised there were no tree nuts involved in their making.

Delia sighed and picked up her sandwich. She'd been sighing a lot lately, both in grief and in resignation to her bizarre situation. Somehow, she didn't see either changing any time soon.

When she finished with her breakfast, she tidied up, then went to the door and chose another cardigan. She didn't stop to sniff the patchouli. She did, however, pat her pocket to make sure her keys were in there before locking the door behind her on the way out. She wanted to do a little gardening, but she no longer felt safe leaving the house open when she wasn't in it. Hell, she didn't feel safe when she *was* in it, locked or not.

She'd just worked up enough body heat to debate taking off the cardigan when her phone buzzed in her pocket. She took off one gardening glove, assuming the text would be from Mom or Julie, but it wasn't.

> I SEE YOU

Her blood froze, and she looked around wildly, scanning the tree line and the dim corners of the yard for someone lurking. She felt exposed suddenly, as if she'd walked directly into the crosshairs.

Her phone buzzed again in her hand, and she dropped it, nervous as a minefield defuser who just heard a click underfoot. It landed in a pile of dirt, and she hurriedly fished it out with shaking hands.

> COPS WON'T SAVE YOU NEXT TIME

The sound of gravel crunching in her driveway had her dropping her phone again. It buzzed in the dirt, and she stared down at the new message.

> SEE YOU SOON

The hum of an engine cut off, and a car door opened, then closed loudly. She snatched up her phone and ran around to the front of the house. Cop car. She stumbled to a stop with a hand on her racing heart.

"Miss Jameson?" A cop she didn't recognize hesitated, hand hovering near his belt, not quite over his gun. "Is there a problem?"

Her breath rushed out of her, leaving her light-headed with relief. "Yes. I just got some scary texts. I'm so glad you're here. Maybe you can do something with the number?"

"Let me see."

She hurried over to him, holding her phone out until he took it. Then, she crossed her arms over her chest, huddling in the cardigan, all her prior warmth completely gone. She felt like she'd been dipped in ice water.

"Did you see anyone on the grounds? In the trees?"

She shook her head. "No one."

"It's probably the guy's sick idea of a joke, but I don't like it. Would you like to ride with me to the station? We can have a tech download the messages and number and see what they can find."

She wanted to say yes, yes she would like to ride in a nice, safe police cruiser to the nice, safe police station where she didn't feel like she was about to be sniped and join GeeGee in dying facedown in the garden. Instead, she pulled herself together.

"I'll definitely follow you in, but I need to run an errand in town anyway, so I'll drive, if that's okay?" She frowned. "Wait, what were you doing here? Is something wrong?"

"Oh, right. Officer Jenkins sent me out to introduce myself since he's off today. He just wanted to make sure you knew the on-duty in case something else happened."

"Oh. That was thoughtful of him." Part of her was suspicious, but she tried to push that part down. "And you are...?"

"Officer Taliferro, Miss Jameson." He touched a finger to his cap. "The whole department knows what's going on, so don't you worry. We're still tracking down Mr. Sullivan, but we'll find him soon."

Now she understood why she felt so suspicious. If she was just plain Miss Jameson who didn't live at The Hollows and hadn't just inherited her great grandaunt's wealth, would she be getting this royal, personal treatment? She didn't think so. Part of her wanted to be angry about that. GeeGee would be incensed at the blatant favoritism of the rich.

Or would she? Were any of GeeGee's feelings real, including offense? Or were they all performative to hide the things she didn't, couldn't feel?

This was so not the time to think about that, though.

Forcing a smile, Delia reached out a hand to shake. "Just Delia, please, Officer Taliferro, and thank you. I'll… uh… just go get my truck's keys."

She needed to put the new keys on her keychain, she decided as she tromped up the steps to the porch. In fairness, she'd only had the truck keys for less than a day, but she should've already done the deed. Annoyed at herself, she grimly worked the key onto her plain little keyring before walking back out the door, locking it firmly behind her.

"Ready."

"If you'll just follow me, ma'am."

"Will do."

She had no idea where the police station was in Webster Groves, so she was glad he hadn't asked to follow her. Lola rumbled like a diesel engine when she keyed the ignition, and she felt a little of that got-wheels freedom flow back into her as she eased up the clutch and smoothly followed the police cruiser down her twisty driveway. It felt good to just drive. She hadn't realized in California how much she'd missed it.

Soon enough, though, she pulled into a parking spot next to

Taliferro's cruiser, then followed him into the building. He led her through a maze of open office desks to a little hallway in the back. The station's IT department looked like it was built in a cave for all the natural light that made it from the glass front of the station down the pokey little hall.

Which was about right, Delia thought as she remembered her own cubicle, which had been about as far from natural light as earth was from the sun.

Thus, she was grinning slightly as Taliferro introduced her to Officer Stephens, who asked her very politely for her phone, which she gave over gladly.

"Please, sit down, if you can find a place." The officer, a sturdy woman with a slightly husky voice and black hair raked back sharply from her face, gestured toward a file-covered chair in the corner. "This should only take a few minutes. We're not doing a full dump."

Delia huffed, moving aside the files and perching on the slightly rickety chair. "I work in IT, too, so I definitely understand not having anywhere to sit."

"Oh, really?" Stephens plugged her phone into something and tapped a few keys on her keyboard. "What type of IT?"

"Internet company Help Desk."

"Ouch."

"Exactly."

They fell quiet while her phone did its thing. Delia felt no urge to make conversation. She was too busy with all the thoughts she'd tried to outdrive.

Someone had her number. Luke, obviously, but also Elijah. In fact, the texts hadn't started until after she'd given him her number. Was that important, or just a coincidence? Did she believe in coincidences anymore?

Unknown.

"Got 'em." Stephens nodded, eyes fixed on her screen. "It's a burner number, but I'm guessing you already knew that. We'll have to send this info to St. Louis to see if they can track down who bought it. I doubt they were dumb enough to use a credit card to buy it, but they would've needed a credit card for payment to activate it, and maybe they were dumb enough to use theirs then."

"How long do you think that'll take?"

Stephens shot her a sympathetic look. "Days, probably. Maybe a week. It's not a fast process, unfortunately. They have a much higher crime rate than we do."

She was disappointed but not surprised, so she just nodded. "I get it."

The cop unplugged her phone and handed it back over. "Keep it charged, and keep it close to hand at all times. If some sicko is after you, this is your lifeline."

She nodded again, accepting her phone and tucking it into her jeans pocket. "Thank you, Officer Stephens."

"No problem. Be careful out there, Miss Jameson."

Delia searched out Officer Taliferro before leaving, just to make sure he didn't need anything else from her, then left the police station with foreboding. She felt marginally better huddled inside the heavy bulk of her truck, but that in-the-crosshairs feeling came back with a vengeance as she walked across the parking lot into the grocery store. Was someone watching her, maybe with binoculars? Had someone followed her into town? Where was Luke? Where was Elijah?

Moving more quickly than she normally would, she tossed a big canister of oats into her cart, thinking of her mother coming for the weekend. Mom liked oatmeal for breakfast, especially with blueberries. Delia had already passed the produce section, so she turned around halfway through the store to go back. She decided on some peaches for herself while she was there, then headed back for the middle of the store and continued on through the aisles.

Cod for lunch, she thought, though she wasn't overly fond of fish herself. It was a compromise between her mother's love of salmon and Delia's love of not eating fish at all. What to eat with baked fish? Pulling her cart aside, she pulled out her phone and Googled. Rice pilaf seemed to be a common side with cod, so she picked a recipe and made sure she had everything on the list. And corn on the cob, of course, but she already had corn on the cob. She'd just picked the last four ears yesterday morning.

When she finally had everything on her mental list, she pushed her cart up to the front, then stood in line, looking with new dread at the windowed front of the store looking out on the parking lot. Was someone out there searching for her right now? Did they see her? Would they start texting her and get her all freaked out in public?

Her phone stayed silent in her jeans pocket, thankfully, and she was able to pay and escape without any fuss. She loaded up Lola, took her cart back to the little corral, then climbed into Lola's cab and again felt marginally safer. She didn't roll down the window on the ride home, though. She wanted to feel closed in. She wasn't free, and she didn't feel like faking it right now.

She eyed the house as she pulled around the last twist in the driveway, and she was relieved when it looked exactly the same as when she'd left. No missing screens, except the one the police had taken away last night. No broken windows. The door was nice and closed, everything right and tight.

Pulling around the back of the house, she got as close to the back door as possible so she wouldn't have to haul groceries too far, then keyed off the engine and jumped down out of the cab. She pulled out her keys and unlocked the door, relieved that it was still locked, then started hauling in grocery bags. When she was done, she took great satisfaction in locking herself inside.

For what it was worth, she was home safe. How long that feeling lasted, though, was entirely up for grabs.

Sighing again, Delia started putting away her groceries.

26

"Oh, Cordie, honey." Mom's voice was heavy with sympathy and worry. "I should start that way right now. I'm already packed. I could just jump in the car."

Delia shook her head, pacing GeeGee's bedroom while she spoke on the phone. "No way, Mom. It's already almost dark. You'd spend almost the whole trip with headlights blinding you. And I don't want you hitting a deer. No." She shook her head, even though she knew her mother wouldn't see it. "You stay put until tomorrow morning. I'll be fine. I've practically got the police on speed dial."

"I'm just so sorry this is happening, honey. This should be a time of healing for you, and instead, you're worried sick. I can hear it in your voice."

"I am worried," Delia admitted, shoving her free hand into her back pocket. "But all the doors and windows are locked, and the police know something hinky is happening. I'll be fine tonight, and you'll be here tomorrow. It's fine."

Mom made unhappy noises, but she eventually agreed. "Okay, but you keep your phone *in your hand,* okay? Don't even put it in your pocket. I want your finger on the button."

She smiled a little. "I don't think that'll work, Mom, but I'll do what I can."

"Good. Be so careful, honey. I'll see you tomorrow. And call if anything else happens, okay?"

"Okay." She wanted to sigh, but she didn't want her mother to hear it. "Love you."

"Love you, too, Cordie. Goodnight."

"Goodnight."

She hung up, then swiped to Julie's number, knowing she'd never hear the end of it if she didn't call and give her friend the scoop right now. Just as she was about to tap the button, her phone buzzed with a text that popped up on the screen.

> Are you okay? I heard there was more trouble earlier. This is Eli, by the way. Do you need me to come over? I get off work in half an hour.

SHE ROLLED HER EYES. EVEN IF SHE DIDN'T HALF-SUSPECT HIM OF being her intruder, she wouldn't want a strange man in her house as the sun was going down. And, old friend or not, he was a stranger now. She barely recognized the accomplished gentleman in the business suit as the devil-may-care youth she used to pal around with during summer break.

She no longer knew him, and she'd do well to remember that, despite her feelings of relief earlier at knowing someone close by had her number and could more easily come to her rescue. She had to be on her guard. For all intents and purposes, she was a woman on her own, newly wealthy, and she was unprepared for the pitfalls that came with that situation.

So she ignored the text and swiped back to Julie's number, then put her phone to her ear. She heard three rings and was mentally preparing a voice mail when Julie answered, sounding out of breath.

"Delia? What's up?"

She blinked. "Are you exercising or something?"

A breathless huff. "I had to run to the break room. I'm working an extra shift today."

"Oh, sorry." Delia had assumed the usual 3:00 AM to 3:00 PM shift and had only hoped to catch her friend before she took her usual afternoon nap. "I can call back some other time if—"

"No way. What's going on? You'd usually just text."

Julie knew her too well.

"Yeah, I know, but a lot has happened. Someone's been breaking into the house, and now I'm getting creepy text messages." She thought back, then stood up a little straighter. "Including one that just said *HI,* all caps, no punctuation. And, more weird than that, someone put all my garden stuff back in the basket when I was out of the room. How creepy is that?"

"Cordelia Jameson, you'd better have called the police."

She huffed at the full name treatment. "I did, I promise. They're treating me like they can't afford to lose my tax revenue."

That earned a rueful snort. "I'll bet, but I'll take it if it keeps you safe from that lunatic."

"Lunatic?" She frowned. "What lunatic?"

"Luke, of course. Isn't he who's stalking you?"

Unable to resist, Delia sighed and sat down on the edge of GeeGee's bed. "Well, maybe, but it could also be a childhood summer friend who knows I'm here, too. Hell, if it's just a matter of who knows I'm here, it could be the Uber driver from the other day, or even my neighbor, Mr. Brinkley. Maybe he wants the property or something."

"This ain't Scooby Doo," Julie protested, though she sounded amused. "My bet is Luke. But tell me more about this childhood friend."

"Ugh." She shook her head. "Platonic only, I promise. We used to hang out when I visited GeeGee over the summer, but I don't know him at all now. He's an accountant, when he used to be all about being a champion rock climber. I thought he'd move to the Grand Canyon or somewhere with cliffs to climb."

Rock climber. He could have figured out a quick parkour-style way to get out her bedroom window to the ground without breaking a leg.

She shook the thought away.

"Anyway, I bumped into him at a store, and then he showed up on my porch."

"Okay, that's creepy. Did you brandish a shotgun and warn him away?"

Amused, she smiled. "I don't have a shotgun. GeeGee didn't like them. She always said the only violence she could get behind was firebombing the NRA headquarters."

"Wow. I really do love that lady."

Delia bit her lower lip and didn't comment. She still loved GeeGee, too. It was so hard to reconcile all the murder in the diary with the GeeGee she thought she knew. Impossible, really. It didn't compute. Blue Screen of Death.

Again, she shook the thought away.

"So yeah, it could technically be him. All this stuff started happening after he saw me at the store, so he definitely knew I was in town. And half the town probably knows I inherited, so he may just be after the money."

"I don't like it. You said someone broke in twice?"

Sheepish, she scratched at her bent elbow. "Weeeellllllll... I sort of didn't lock the windows, even after I started locking the doors."

"Delia!"

"I know! My only excuse is this is the country. We don't lock up here, okay?"

"I hope you're locking everything up to and including your underwear drawer now."

She chuckled. "That's a big ten-four. Everything locked and accounted for."

"Good."

A little quiet fell until Delia remembered that Julie was at work and would likely need to be back soon.

"Mom's coming tomorrow, so I won't be here alone for a couple of days."

"Good." This time, the word held a world of relief. "Maybe he'll leave you alone."

"I hope so."

"Look, I gotta get back."

"I know." Delia stood up off the bed. "Thanks for listening to me ramble, Jules. I needed that."

"You keep me posted on all of this nonsense, you hear?"

"I hear."

"Okay. Love you."

"You, too. Bye."

Julie hung up without another word, and Delia paced around the room again before settling down into the wingback for more reading. She'd brought in an oracle card from a deck GeeGee never really liked to use as a bookmark. It was the Introspection card, which she thought applied. Surely, GeeGee would approve.

Why she still cared what GeeGee would think, she'd never know.

Sighing, she started to read.

27

A merry Yule was had by all. The family still hates that I call it Yule instead of Christmas. They mumble about Satan worship instead of Wicca. I've stopped explaining that it's earth magic, not demon worship, but then I wonder why I care. And then I discovered I don't care. Let them think what they want.

I do what I want.

Delia found herself nodding, again reluctantly agreeing with her murderous great grandaunt. She, too, celebrated Yule instead of Christmas, and she didn't even count herself a Wiccan. She just liked sticking it in people's craw.

A side effect of being nurtured by a serial killer? Unknown.

My brother's new wife is already pregnant. He has two teenage sons and a ten-year-old daughter already, but that's what you get when your second wife is younger than the first was when you first married

her. He's a fool, but he's also a darling, and I love him. As much as I love anything or anyone.
    I would never harm him. It would hurt me to do so. Is that love? I like to think so.
    More interestingly, one of my men was discovered yesterday. It made national news, as it turns out he was some minor politician in his state's legislature. I probably should have known that, given how obnoxious he'd been, but I was on vacation. I'm always on vacation when I take my men.
    Don't shit where you eat.

DELIA SAT UP SO SUDDENLY THAT SHE ALMOST DROPPED THE diary. GeeGee's vacations. Surely, the woman wasn't killing someone every time she took a trip to another state? Even to other countries? And the occasional cruise, despite the earlier talk of death and food poisoning.

Sick, she tried to tally up the possible kill total based on at least two vacations per year since Delia had been aware of GeeGee's love of travel. Just in her own lifetime, that could be fifty victims. Surely not. Surely not so many.

She wanted to get up and pace. Instead, she looked down at the diary and almost unwillingly read the next lines.

    They assume he had some sort of health event while camping in the deep woods on conservation land. That's certainly where I left him with a tent and a sleeping bag. He thought we would have a romantic tryst in the gentle forest. We did not.
    A stroke, they think, or a heart attack, but he's quite decomposed. Bones and rags. It's been years, after all. There's no heart or brain left to tell for sure. I hid him well.
    I've started buying land.

. . .

DELIA BLINKED AND LEANED BACK INTO THE WINGBACK'S comfortable embrace. The thought seemed to come out of nowhere, when GeeGee was otherwise so logically point to point. It was jarring.

I bought the land where I hid my first, of course. I always intended to. But I've looked far afield, too, to my favorite states to visit. No one would be surprised if I perhaps wanted to build houses where I like to stay.
No one will ever know they are my own private killing fields.

EVERYTHING INSIDE HER SEEMED TO SINK INTO THE FLOOR. ALL those properties GeeGee had accumulated over the years. Surely not... it couldn't be....

I can no longer trust in wild, out of the way areas. Communities are becoming quite good at massive searches these days, you see. And even on conservation lands, it's clearly possible that a ranger will stumble across a body, even far afield. And I don't trust hotel staff to not conveniently remember a dead man going up to his room with a strange woman when asked later by the police. A few times at different hotels, yes, but never the same hotel twice.
You can't be too careful. Better to have private property. Less likely to be randomly searched or be randomly remembered that way later. Safer.
As long as I don't leave together with my kill, I should be completely safe on my own land.

. . .

Delia deliberately placed the oracle card, closed the diary, and put it on the little stand by the chair. Then, she stood up and walked directly out of the room. She felt like bursting into a run, but where the hell could she go?

She needed... tea. No, that wasn't soothing enough. A hot bath? Yes. That's exactly what she needed. A hot bath and a good night's sleep. She was so, so tired from all the stress and her lost night's sleep. Several nights now, actually. Her body ached with exhaustion. She hadn't even eaten supper.

She needed to take better care of herself. She even had the money to do so now, so there was no excuse.

As she soaked in the tub, she heard her phone buzz a couple of times with text messages. Elijah, perhaps? She'd forgotten to text him back and, frankly, didn't think he warranted a text back just yet. Julie? She might be off work by now. Mom?

Luke?

Sighing, she washed wearily, then stood up out of the tub, climbing out carefully. She took her time drying off. It had only been three texts, after all, and spaced apart. No one was burning up her phone trying to reach her.

When she finally had her kimono wrapped around her still damp body, she went to the vanity, picked up her phone, and felt suddenly frozen through.

KNOCK KNOCK

KNOCK KNOCK

KNOCK KNOCK

"Oh, shit."

She spun on her bare heel and headed for the bathroom door, her finger already scrolling to the emergency button. As she opened the door, she heard two deliberate knocks on her bedroom door and almost fell over trying to stop her forward momentum.

Heavy footsteps pounded down the hallway, then down the stairs. The front door opened. Slammed shut.

Silence.

Delia stood there, three steps outside her steamy bathroom, barefoot and only wearing a damp kimono, and tried to think. Tried to move, to function in any way. But she couldn't.

How long had he been standing outside her bedroom door, waiting for the inner door to open? How had he gotten in? She knew for a fact that she'd locked all the doors and checked all the windows before settling down with the diary earlier.

And why? How would this end in money for a stalker? *Was* it about money?

Weak at the knees, she eventually stumbled over to her bed and sat down on the corner, huddling in her chilly kimono. Pointless to call for help. He was already gone. She could report the incident in the morning, but there was no sense calling the whole damn force out tonight. Surely, he wouldn't be back.

Would he?

Maybe she should call what's-his-name, Taliferro, after all. Maybe they'd send another cop to sit in her driveway all night. Would that make her feel safer?

It wasn't even nine o'clock yet, and she hadn't slept much at all last night. Would she sleep better with a cop in her driveway? She just didn't know. She didn't know anything. She was too freaked out.

He'd been standing outside her bedroom door. Just standing there, waiting for her to leave the bathroom to scare her. Somehow, that was more terrifying than anything else. The patience of it.

I should've chased him, she thought, her shoulders squaring, her back stiffening. I could've caught a glimpse, something. Why didn't I chase him?

Resolved, she lifted her nearly forgotten phone and swiped to her browser, looking for the non-emergency police line. She didn't need lights and sirens. She just needed to report what had happened, and she would accept the offer of an officer on her property if it was offered. Right now, at this moment, she almost hoped her stalker would be back.

She wasn't as helpless as she sometimes thought herself.

Her unknown stalker would find that out the hard way.

28

"You look tired," Mom said as she climbed out of the car before lunch the next morning. "Rough night?"

Delia fought a sigh and a yawn. Officer Taliferro had insisted on coming out himself to look around, despite her protests that he wouldn't find anything. He didn't, of course. He did, however, volunteer to stay in her driveway until dawn, and Delia had agreed. Thus, she'd managed a few hours of sleep, but apparently, not enough.

"I'm fine." She was, mostly. "Do you need some help with your bag?"

"Oh, yes, thank you, Cordie. Tell me what's been going on."

As she'd rather do almost anything but that, Delia picked up the little travel case and headed for the steps up to the porch. Her mother trailed along behind, and Delia could feel eyes boring into her back.

She gave in, but only a little bit. "I just got some more weird texts last night. I'd block the number, but I want to give the info to the police so maybe they can find him."

"Honey, that's no good. Did you call the police?"

Huffing a little as she hauled the heavy little case up the

steps, she again hedged her bets. "I did. They're looking into it. Let's not talk about it anymore, okay?"

"All right, Cordie. I'm sorry."

She sighed and put the case down on its rolly wheels when she reached the porch. "Don't be sorry, Mom. I'm just a little stressed out right now."

"For good reason. And still grieving, too." She put a hand on Delia's arm. "You've lost so much weight, honey. You've been through so much the past several months, and now all of this. I'm just so sorry."

Overcome by the sincerity on her mother's face, Delia leaned in for a lingering hug and let herself unwind a bit. She and her mother didn't always get along, but she never doubted she was loved or that she loved in return.

I would never harm him. It would hurt me to do so. Is that love?

She shook the words away, abruptly pulling out of her mother's arms. She didn't want to think about the diaries right now. She'd carefully hidden 1981 away without picking up 1982, arranging the dresses before the trunk so no one would ever guess it was there. She didn't want Mom to go looking for something and accidentally discover them.

She still didn't know what she would do with the diaries when she finished reading them. Honestly, that was so far down on her back burner that it wasn't even lukewarm.

"I have stuff all laid out to make some lunch. I've never baked cod before, but I found a supposedly fool-proof recipe online. Is rice pilaf and corn on the cob okay? I can do other vegetables, if you want."

"Cordie, honey, you're rambling."

"I know." She closed her eyes and took a deep breath. "Sorry. Just... let's go eat some lunch."

"All right, honey. I'll help you bake the fish. One less thing to worry about."

Smiling a little, though the last thing she wanted was to eat fish on such an unsettled stomach, Delia opened the front door and ushered her mother inside, then locked the door behind them. She had to be sure, though it hadn't seemed to matter last night.

Nope. Not thinking about that right now.

"Do you want to get settled first, or do you want to eat first?"

Mom looked around the foyer, and it occurred to Delia that she'd only been here a handful of times over the years, and the last time had likely been a good decade. To Delia, the house never changed, but she supposed it must have in that span of time. What must Mom think of the place?

"I suppose you could show me to a room, and then we can cook and talk a little before we eat. Does that sound alright?"

"Of course. Make yourself at home."

Not in GeeGee's room, of course. One of the guest rooms upstairs would do. Her mother's knees weren't the best, but they'd survive a few trips up and down the stairs.

"Here, let's get you to a room."

She led the way upstairs, going into the first door down the hall toward her own bedroom. It wasn't a gabled room, like hers, but it was roomy and bright for all of that. She'd put fresh sheets, a bedspread, and a quilt on the bed this morning. She was grateful for the quilt because the only bedspread she could find that fit the full-size bed sported a huge floral pattern in shades of mauve, where the walls were a rather lovely shade of robin's egg blue. The quilt, though, was a beautiful crazy quilt hodgepodge and would have matched any room in the house.

"What a lovely bedspread," Mom said as she caught sight of it hanging longer than the quilt. "Why on earth did you cover it up with that old quilt?"

Delia didn't shake her head, nor did she sigh. "You can switch them if you want, but it's cold enough at night that you'll want both."

"No, it's fine, honey. This is a lovely room. Thank you."

"*Mi casa es su casa.*"

Her mother didn't comment, but Delia could feel an awkwardness there that she didn't understand. Now that this was her place, surely Mom knew she was welcome any time... didn't she?

Then again, Delia still didn't feel like the place was hers, so maybe it wasn't too surprising that Mom didn't feel like she could just barge in any old time.

"Where's the bathroom?"

"Oh, right across the hall." She led the way back into the hall and opened the door directly across. "My bathroom is right through the wall."

"I remember now. It's just been a while since I was upstairs."

Which was true. If it had been a decade since Mom had been here at all, it had been longer still since she'd been upstairs where Delia stayed. It wasn't off-limits, by any means, but since she was the only one who stayed with any regularity, it often felt like the upstairs was Delia's and the downstairs was GeeGee's.

"Do you want a minute to settle in?"

"Yes, if you don't mind, honey. I need to powder my nose."

Delia grinned at the antiquated phrase, but it was Mom right down to the ground. Never be direct when a euphemism would do.

"No problem. Do you remember where the kitchen is?"

"I'll find it."

"Okay. I'll be in the kitchen, then. Take your time."

She left her mother at the door to the bathroom and went downstairs, where she checked the door to make sure it was still locked before heading into the kitchen. The cod was on the counter, coming up to room temperature. Corn on the cob was cut into chunks and ready for boiling in seasoned water. Rice pilaf was ready to be sauteed before going into the steamer. She should probably tackle it first, as the cod wouldn't take as long to cook. First, though, she turned on the oven to preheat.

She'd just transferred the sizzling, golden-brown, buttery rice and orzo pasta to the steamer when Mom made her way in and offered to help.

"What can I do?"

Delia gestured toward her phone, which was over by the cod on the counter. "Can you take a look at that recipe and see if it sounds good?"

"Sure." She made a few hmming noises and nodded a few times. Eventually, she put the phone down. "That sounds like a perfectly good recipe. Do you want me to get started on it while you do the corn?"

"Absolutely." Delia could not be more excited to not have to touch raw fish. "Although it's kind of a bad deal. I literally just have to bring the water to a boil."

"You made the pilaf, honey." But Mom sounded distracted as she shook seasonings onto the cod filets. "Besides, this will just take a second."

Delia heard clanking and turned to see her mother whipping the herbs and lemon juice she'd laid out into the softened butter with a fork, really putting her back into it. She grinned, then hid the expression. Trust Mom to attack the recipe like her life depended on it.

Once the herbed butter mix was done, they both slathered it onto the cod, coating both sides, then placed the filets in a nice little casserole dish Delia had found in GeeGee's baking dish cabinet. Then, into the oven.

"There. Do you want some tea? I know you like GeeGee's Blue Butterfly mix."

Mom perked up. "Yes, that would be lovely, dear. Where do you keep the tea things?"

"I got it. Why don't you go sit in the window nook and survey the kingdom? I'll bring it over when it's steeping."

When she'd settled at the little table, Mom sighed. "This really is a lovely property, isn't it? GeeGee did a beautiful job on the landscaping."

Delia nodded, feeling a nostalgia that had been robbed from her in the past days and clinging to it desperately. "She really did. She was one hell of a gardener."

"Mm." Mom was quiet a moment, then stirred. "What beautiful wind chimes. What are those sparkly rocks?"

"Selenite crystal points," Delia said wryly, knowing her mother wouldn't appreciate her amusement but unable to help herself. "It's a goddess stone that brings protection."

"Mm." That didn't sound nearly as contented as the first one. "Well, it's just lovely."

The water boiled in the electric kettle, so Delia poured it over the tea in the pot, then popped on the lid and rooted around for another teacup. She chose the one with pale roses all over it, remembering that her mother had liked the mauve flowers on the bedspread.

Then, they settled together at the little table and waited for the tea to steep while looking out the window. It was a nice, quiet moment, and Delia cherished it. She'd had so few of those in the past few days. The past months, really.

Years? Possibly.

"Have you decided to live here, Cordie?" Mom watched as Delia poured the tea. "You know you're always welcome back home. I'd love having you closer, but this is so much better than California."

Slowly, she nodded as she breathed in the beautiful, floral aroma of the tea, soothed by its lovely blue shade in her cup.

"The property is in my name now, and I'll have the money to keep it up, so I think I'll probably stay here. I know it's not as close as you want, but… it's mine now."

Although she also owned who knew how many veritable graveyards full of GeeGee's victims, but she did not want to think about that. Soothing blue tea. Lovely floral scent. Breathe, Delia.

Mom nodded, not looking terribly disappointed. "I understand. You were always so happy here."

She lifted her cup for a sip, then paused at a knock on the door. For a split second, her blood ran cold. Then, almost as quickly, she was suffused with anger. How dare he. How *dare* he fuck with her while her mother was here.

"Cordie? Honey, what's wrong? Who is that?"

"Wait here, Mom."

Without waiting to see if her mother would follow that barked order, Delia jerked up out of her chair and stormed into the foyer. She yanked open the lock, then flung open the door, prepared to cannonball herself out onto the porch and in full chase of whoever dared to fuck with her when she had such delicate company.

"Oh, hey—"

"Elijah?" she demanded incredulously, her hands already shaking from the adrenaline rush and her need to defend herself and her mother. "What the hell—"

"I know, I know, I said I'd text before just showing up again, but I saw the strange car and that old truck and I got worried, and—"

She grunted, not caring if it sounded unladylike. "You just happened to be in my curvy-ass driveway far enough to see strange vehicles?"

His cheeks flushed, and he scruffed his hand through his hair. "Yeah, okay. I was coming to see you, but I promise I just wanted to ask you to dinner again. But then I really did get worried and wanted to check on you."

Gritting her teeth, she resisted the urge to call him a creepy stalker and threaten to call the cops on him, like she had Luke. "Elijah, you really should have texted or even called. But to set your mind at ease, I'm fine, that's my old truck, and that's my mother's car."

"Hello? Is everything okay out here?"

Delia sighed. Of course her mother would disregard her order to stay back.

"It's fine, Mom. It's just Elijah."

Mom perked up. "Elijah? Isn't that the nice young man you used to talk about playing with during your summers here?"

Now, it was Delia's turn to blush. "Mom!"

"That's me, ma'am. I guess we've never officially met." Elijah started to offer his hand, then realized Delia hadn't moved out of the way yet. "Elijah Campbell, ma'am, though everyone else just calls me Eli."

An apology trembled on the tip of her tongue, but Delia didn't say it. He'd shown up unexpectedly yet again, even knowing she was having problems that required police intervention. The least he could do was show her the courtesy of not giving her yet another reason to distrust him.

"Well, Eli, it's very nice to meet you. I'm Cordie's mother, Carolyn." She deliberately nudged Delia out of the way so she could offer her own hand to the newcomer. "Cordie has told me so much about you."

He took the offered hand, shaking very gently. "Recently?"

"Well, no. I take it it's been some time since you two last saw each other."

"It's been some years, ma'am."

"Well, please, come in. We're about to have lunch, if you'd like to join us."

Delia gritted her teeth together. The last thing she wanted was Eli Campbell crowding up to her little table in the window nook, but she'd be damned if she moved the whole lot to the dining room. Baked cod and rice pilaf wasn't fancy enough for the full dining room treatment, and frankly, neither was the company.

"Oh, I hate to be a bother. I really was just stopping by to see if Delia wanted to get some cashew chicken at that place we used to go back in the day."

Despite herself, she scoffed. "That place is still open?"

"It's even expanded. What do you say? Dinner tonight? Maybe seven o'clock?"

"She'd love to," Mom said, smiling. "She needs the distraction, and I'm so relieved to know that a nice, strapping young man like yourself is nearby with all of this hullabaloo going on."

"Mom!"

"Done. Meet you there? Do you remember how to get there?"

"Yes, but—"

"Great. It's settled then. I'll see you tonight."

"It was nice to meet you, Eli." Mom waved him off the porch, all smiles. "Thank you for stopping by."

"No problem, Miss Carolyn. Enjoy your lunch."

"We will." Mom turned a serene smile toward Delia, then frowned. "What?"

"What if he's the creepy stalker, Mother? Jesus!"

"Oh, Cordie, I don't think that nice young man you used to talk about would ever scare you like that. I'm sure he's not the one."

She threw up her hands. "He's been acting weird since I got here! Why didn't you ask me before selling me at auction?"

"Oh, honey, don't be upset. You need to get out and get your mind off all of this scary business for a while. I'm an excellent judge of character, and that young man seems very nice to me."

"Of course he seems nice! They always seem nice just before they sneak into your house and knock on your bedroom door while you're naked in the bathroom!"

"What?" Mom was aghast. "Oh, Cordie, honey, did that happen? Well, no wonder you're all wound up."

"Of course I'm wound up!"

"Shh, shh." Coming closer, Mom made soothing gestures until she could put gentle hands on Delia's arms. "I won't ask why you didn't tell me, but honey, you can't go on like this. What do the police say?"

Suddenly miserable, Delia sagged. "They're practically tripping over themselves to spend the night in my driveway, but that's only because I'm rich people now. If I wasn't, they probably wouldn't even believe me."

"Honey, that's not true."

No, it wasn't, but it felt true.

"I'm just so tired, Mom," Delia admitted, closing her eyes. "So tired. I don't know how much more of this shit I can take."

Her mother engulfed her in a hug, smoothing a hand up and down her back under her hair. Annoyingly, Delia felt on the verge of tears, yet again. It had been a few days since she really let herself cry, and she suddenly felt cheated out of her grief on top of everything else. Between the diary and the stalker, she'd been kicked right out of the grief cycle and sailed right past healing. She felt like she'd never be right again.

"Go ahead, honey. Let it out."

She didn't want to, but with her mother hugging her close, she couldn't help it. Wrapping her arms around her mother's small form, Delia let herself go.

She cried for a long, long time.

29

"I'm so glad you made it," Eli said, pulling out a chair for her. Delia tried not to judge that move as pretentious, given that they were just at a Chinese buffet. The place *had* spruced up a bit over the years, but it was still Chinese buffet in a small town. Definitely not a place that demanded a business suit and pulling out the chair for the lady.

The lady who, by the way, was in jeans and a flannel shirt with a long-sleeved t-shirt underneath.

"Yeah, well, between you and my mom, I wasn't sure I had a choice. She practically kicked me out of the house."

Eli's expression went carefully, politely blank. "Good. You're dealing with a lot just since you've been here. I bet a million bucks you needed to get out and think about something else for a while."

She sighed. "You sound like Mom."

"She sounds like a smart woman." He picked up his menu, which was a joke, since they would both likely be eating off the buffet. Who even looked at a menu at any buffet place? "So how much of the rumor is true?"

Raising one eyebrow, she stared at him. "What rumor?"

Jesus, she'd only been in town for less than a week. How were there already rumors about her?

"That Miss Virginia left you her whole fortune."

Her eyes narrowed, and she felt herself stiffening. Maybe the break-ins were about money, after all. How would anyone even know? Were wills not confidential? She supposed they were for the lawyers, but maybe not for the people who did or didn't benefit from them. Dammit.

"Is that a yes?"

She grunted, well past the thought of being ladylike. "Not her whole fortune, no."

"But a lot."

"Can we not talk about this?"

"Sorry. Just making small talk until the server comes to take our orders."

Delia gritted her teeth together. "Are we not just getting the buffet?"

"They make a mean mayonnaise shrimp."

"That sounds revolting."

"Wow." Eli finally let go of his mask to look at her with surprising sympathy. "This week really *has* been rough on you, hasn't it?"

Her shoulders slumped. "Or am I, as you're starting to suspect, just a mean, caustic bitch these days?"

"I wasn't thinking that."

"I was." She sighed. "Look, I'm sorry, okay? I'm under a lot of pressure right now, and I'm not handling it very well. And I'm so damn tired."

He nodded sympathetically. "I'll bet. You've been on the police band more times than I can count."

She rubbed her eyes with one hand. "That's only half of it."

"What's the other half?"

But she'd already said too much, so she reverted to pushing him away. "Forget it. Let's just get this over with."

If she didn't know better, she'd swear he looked genuinely hurt. She felt a little bit bad and again tried to soften her sharp edges.

"How goes the accounting world?"

He was spared having to answer by a waiter sailing over in a smart Chinese suit done in blues. Eli ordered the mayonnaise shrimp, so Delia hurriedly looked at the menu and chose crispy honey chicken so she wouldn't look like a horse let loose in the grain bin over at the buffet. When the waiter left, a little quiet fell between them. Delia felt no urge to fill it.

Frankly, it was nice to just be quiet for a moment.

"How was California, really?"

His tone was so gentle that she didn't shoot him down. Besides, despite the shitty job and the heartache, California was a pretty safe topic. So, she shrugged.

"Expensive. Beautiful, but expensive. And I wasn't really in the beautiful part."

He nodded. "I'm surprised you didn't come up with your own start-up while you were out there. You were always the smart one. You absolutely murdered me at every video game we ever played."

She almost flinched at the word "murdered", but the rest just made her feel sad. If she was so smart, how had she made so many wrong decisions?

"I didn't have anything everyone else out there didn't have," she said, choosing her words carefully. "You take a job at a big internet company, thinking you're gonna make the big bucks later by getting in on the ground floor now, but then you just stay on the ground floor. And out there, you can't afford to live on ground floor wages."

"That sucks."

"It really does." She shrugged. "But it's over now. I've moved back for good, I guess. The Hollows is my home now."

He smiled, his expression magically lightening. "Remember when Miss Virginia did midnight séances, just for us? Man, your mom would've had a cow."

"Why do you think I never told her?" She found herself grinning a little. "What about all that camping out by that grody old pond? Can you believe we swam in that funk?"

"So. Many. Mosquitos." He shook his head. "It was so much nicer when Miss Virginia put in the koi pond instead. And closer to the house in case we changed our minds."

"Or the coyotes got too close."

"Or that."

She chuckled. "How many times did you beat me racing bikes in the driveway?"

"Every time." Not a shade of shame lurked in his tone. "How many times did you wipe out trying to take one of the turns at speed?"

"Every other time, at least." It was her turn to shake her head. "How I ever had skin on my knees, I'll never know. I have scars to this day."

"I'll bet." He smirked. "Sometimes, you gotta go slow to go fast."

"Okay, Grasshopper."

"Grasshopper was the student, not the master."

The waiter returned with their drinks, but it only served to loosen up the mood even more. No alcohol, as they were both driving, but just the reminder that they were in public and should probably not look like they were about to fight.

It helped Delia, anyway.

"Anyway. Good times." Eli took a sip of his iced tea. "I was thinking about that last summer just yesterday."

"Ah." She managed a sad little smile. "You mean the summer I discovered video games were more exciting than camping by the koi pond and you discovered chasing girls was funner than video games?"

"That's the one." He sighed. "I should've been chasing you."

Her eyebrows rose. That was… not what she was expecting. They never had that sort of friendship, as far as she knew.

"Don't give me that look. We were friends. I guess I always thought someday we'd be more than friends."

She frowned. "Why do guys always have to do that? Why can't men and women just be friends without the expectation that it'll be more someday?"

This time, his eyebrows rose. "It wasn't an expectation, Delia. It was a hope."

But she was just getting started. "But why? I was perfectly happy with us being friends. Why couldn't we just stay that way?" She blinked, her mouth dropping open for one regrettable moment. "Jesus, Elijah, is that why you quit hanging around? Because I never considered dating you?"

He very deliberately arranged his fork, napkin, and glass of tea. "Of course not. I just… we were so good together. Why didn't we ever take it further?"

"Because I didn't want to. That's why." She shook her head. "I can't believe you dumped me as a friend because I didn't want to date you."

"I didn't dump you as a friend."

She snorted inelegantly. "Yes, you did. It wasn't me saying I had other plans when you called up. You're the one who didn't want to play video games with me."

"Because you always won!"

"You always won the bike races, but I still raced you!"

"Shh!" He jerked back in his chair, as he'd been practically bent over the table. Looking sheepish suddenly, he looked around to see if anyone had been bothered by their raised voices. "We're gonna get kicked out if we're not careful."

She wanted to snark back with a very adult "So!", but she

restrained herself by crossing her arms over her chest and leaning back in her chair. She couldn't believe what bullshit he'd just dumped in her lap. As if it was *her* fault they weren't friends anymore.

"I'm sorry." He looked like he was gritting his teeth, but he got it out. "I didn't think about you maybe not wanting more than just friendship, okay?"

She refused to apologize. She hadn't done anything wrong. Maybe it was for the best that they'd drifted apart all these years. Right now, it seemed like they'd never had anything in common.

"Delia, I really am sorry. I shouldn't have brought it up." He looked ridiculously sincere. "I've really missed you. Can't we still be friends?"

An equally mature "I dunno, can we?" hovered on the tip of her tongue, but she wrestled it back and sighed.

"Look, Eli. I appreciate you getting back in touch with me now that I'm here. I really do. But if you're looking for more than friendship, I'll tell you right now that I'm still not. I just got out of a bad relationship, and I'm not in any hurry to try my luck again. I have too much going on right now, anyway."

He looked down at the table for a moment, then nodded and looked her in the eye. "Blunt honesty. I guess I can always expect that from you."

"I've never had much patience for subterfuge."

"I know." He sighed. "Okay, Delia. Just friends. I promise."

Mollified, she reluctantly loosened her cross-armed stance. "Good. Thank you."

As if he'd been just waiting for their little tiff to be over, the waiter appeared with their food, placing the plates with practiced grace and bowing as he backed away. Murmuring thanks, they both looked down at their plates. Delia didn't know about Eli, but she was wondering if she was even hungry after all the emotional upheaval.

"Man, this smells good."

She wanted to roll her eyes, but she was afraid it would set them both off again. Instead, she grimly picked up her fork and made herself take a bite.

At which point, she moaned in ecstasy.

"Oh, my god, this is amazing."

"Eh? Didn't I tell you they'd made improvements?"

She ate hugely and without any more upsetting conversation. Luckily, Eli seemed just as enamored of his shrimp. He, too, ate without interrupting the bites with words. For a while, it was rather pleasant. Out of the house, away from the diaries and the stalker.

Unless, of course, Eli was the stalker. Luckily, her crispy honey chicken was too good to worry about that right now.

When they'd both eaten their fill and asked for boxes for the rest, they sat back in their seats and studied each other with new frankness. Delia couldn't help but catalog the differences between the boy she'd known and the man who sat before her. She didn't doubt he was doing the same with her.

"I'm glad you came out tonight, Delia."

She shrugged. "Mom said I was as nervous as a bat on a beach and just about kicked me out the door, so…."

He grinned. "I like your mom."

"Me, too." She huffed. "And she was right. You both were right. I did need some time outside of my head."

He nodded. "We all do sometimes. Dare I suggest we do this again sometime?"

Her eyes narrowed.

"Just as friends. Super swear."

Snorting, she reached for her water and rolled her eyes. "Okay, fine. But text me this time? Please? I'll be jumpy until they catch this guy, so… seriously. No more just showing up."

"I promise."

"Thank you."

The waiter brought their little cardboard takeout boxes with metal handles, so they busied themselves with packing up their leftovers. Small talk was over. Now, there was just a goodbye to be said. Hopefully, he'd keep his promise and keep his hands to himself.

Before she could start the goodbyes, though, he scooted his chair back.

"Do you mind if I take a bathroom break?"

Her eyebrows rose. "No? Take your time."

"Thanks. Be right back."

She shook her head and debated licking her plate while he was gone, but the waiter came over and took them before she could make up her mind. She thanked him and paid for her check, noticing that Eli had left his card in the little folder for his own ticket. Good. No worries about who was paying for whom. To each their own.

She was just stuffing her receipt into her jeans pocket when he returned.

"Are you ready?" he asked, eyebrows raised.

"Ready."

They walked out together, and he walked her to her truck. She started to tense up, then realized he was probably being chivalrous rather than amorous. She did have a stalker on her ass, after all. Even if he was the stalker, he'd have to keep up the appearance of being innocent.

Did she really think he was the one creeping around her house? Surely, Luke was far more likely. But she *had* just given him her number when she started getting suspicious texts….

"You really bought this old thing?"

Her eyebrows went up. "Are you impugning my Lola's reputation?"

"Lola, huh?" He patted the hood. "She looks like a Lola. And no, I was not. I'm more of a Beamer guy myself these days."

"I see." She would have never guessed that of the old Elijah, but she could maybe see it of Eli. "Well, as you can see, I'm still a jeans and flannel kind of girl."

"Nineties kid."

"By the skin of my teeth." She snorted. "Besides, you're the one who had the Nirvana poster on your door, Smells Like Teen Spirit."

"If I remember, you were more of a Red-Hot Chili Peppers girl."

"What can I say? The lead singer is still hot."

He snorted, finally sounding a little like the kid she'd known.

"You're just saying that because he has long hair."

"Yeah? And?"

"Get outta here." He backed away, nearly bumped into a car's rear fender, and put up his hands. "I promise I won't just drop by again."

"Good." She opened the truck's door and climbed inside. "Goodnight, Eli."

"Goodnight, Delia. Drive safe."

"You, too."

"Look out for deer!"

She rolled her eyes but secretly appreciated the reminder. It was almost deer season, when the big nuisances tended to go running hell for leather right in front of running vehicles, so it was a valid concern. She didn't answer back, though, just waved out the back glass.

And then she saw it.

The piece of paper stuck under her windshield wiper.

Taking a deep breath, she rolled down the window, scooted way forward in the seat, and stuck her arm out the window to snatch the paper off her windshield. Then, she turned on the cab light to read it.

I STILL SEE YOU

NOWHERE TO RUN TO BABY
NOWHERE TO HIDE

S HIVERING, SHE KEYED THE TRUCK ON AND CRANKED THE HEATER. She was suddenly freezing.

He went to the bathroom, was all she could think.

He went to the bathroom.

30

Another night of rotten sleep, and this time, Delia didn't dare go down to GeeGee's room and start reading 1982. She didn't want her mother asking questions about what she was doing in her dead great grandaunt's room at ass o'clock in the morning.

Instead, she dragged out of bed just after dawn, took a shower in hopes of bringing some color to her face, then snuck downstairs to start the oatmeal cooking down. Mom was a light sleeper who never slept in, so she doubted she'd beat her out of bed by much. Sure enough, she'd just cut up her own peaches and washed the blueberries when Mom shuffled into the kitchen in a bathrobe and a flannel nightgown, slippers on her feet and a yawn on her lips.

"Good morning."

"Good morning, honey." Mom stretched, then shuffled on over to the window nook and sat down, leaning an elbow on the table like a decadent Philistine. "That smells good."

"It's just oatmeal. Did you want skim milk or 2%?"

"Two percent," Mom said on another yawn. "Do you have any orange juice?"

"I have passionfruit mango juice?"

"Oh. I suppose I could try that."

She didn't sound very sure about the situation, so Delia only poured her half a glass and took both glasses over to the table.

"Blueberries, right?"

"Yes, dear. Thank you." Mom sniffed at the juice, then took a delicate sip. Her eyebrows went up. "Oh, this is nice. I like it. What's it called again?"

Delia grinned and went for the bottle to just show her, as it would be easier than trying to pronounce the fancy name. GeeGee tended to put her money where her mouth was and buy from organic small businesses. She'd funded plenty of them in her heyday, and they'd done well by each other. Delia had just discovered how well from Barrett's email yesterday morning.

Jesus, was that really just yesterday morning?

"I can ship you some if you like it," she offered, not wanting her mother to do without something she liked just because it would be expensive. "I'll be getting myself some more anyway."

"That would be lovely, honey. Thank you."

She made a mental note even as she went back to the stove to scoop them each a nice helping of oatmeal. She added a little milk to each bowl and gave a good stir, then sprinkled on blueberries for her mother and diced peaches for herself. Then, she took both bowls over to the table where Mom sat, dreamily sipping at her juice.

"What a beautiful morning."

Delia, who would have loved to sleep in and make up for so many lost nights' sleep, fought back a snarky comment. "It is. I need to do some stuff in the garden after breakfast. Can you entertain yourself for an hour or so?"

"Oh, I could use the exercise. Why don't I help you?"

She nodded. "Sounds like a plan. I think GeeGee has extra gloves in the shed. Do you have a light coat? There are cardigans by the door if you don't."

"I brought one. It's gotten so chilly the past few days."

They ate their breakfast in companionable quiet, watching the day brighten outside the bank of windows. Delia caught herself watching the wind chimes, though the breeze was never quite enough to make them chime. The dangling selenite points caught the morning sunlight and sparkled like diamonds, throwing off fans of color. Beautiful, really. Had it really jangled the other night?

She surely couldn't have imagined such a clamor. She didn't want to think what it would mean. She didn't want to think about possibly having two stalkers instead of one.

But that reminded her of the note under her wiper last night, and she suddenly didn't want any more of her lovely oatmeal.

She should call in to Taliferro. Or would it be Jenkins today? She didn't know and suddenly didn't care. It didn't matter anyway. As far as she knew, they were nowhere near to catching this guy.

Eli? Or Luke? Or neither? But who else could it be?

"Cordie? Honey?"

"Yeah, Mom?" She shook off her thoughts. "Sorry, what did you say?"

"I asked if you were done with your breakfast. I'll do the dishes."

She forced a little smile, though it didn't have much conviction behind it. "There's a dishwasher. You don't have to do the dishes."

"I'll just give them a little rinse. But you didn't eat very much."

She hurried to take another bite, but the oatmeal had gone unpleasantly cool. Gruel, now, instead of a lovely warm bowl of breakfast.

She stuck to the peaches, instead, and ate them quickly so she could hand off her bowl. Then, she took one last look at the wind chimes before getting up from the table to help her mother tidy up. A sudden thought struck her and she blurted it out before she could rethink the question.

"Could you teach me how to can all of this produce?"

Her mother's face brightened. "Of course, Cordie. Do you have a pressure cooker? Of course you do. You have a garden. We can start right after we're done this morning."

"Great. Thanks, Mom."

"My pleasure, honey."

They worked together to tidy up the kitchen enough to go out to the garden. Mom needed no guidance as to where to best use her talents and went straight for the picking.

"Everything's almost done, isn't it?"

Delia nodded, forking out a weed that had sprung up seemingly overnight in the pumpkin patch. "Just about. It's late in the season. GeeGee was a whiz at keeping stuff growing longer than it usually would, but even she couldn't control the change of the seasons."

Mom hmmed, looking over the gourds and squashes. "Are these delicata?"

She looked over to where her mother was pointing and nodded "They're delicious. Do you want to take some home with you? I can definitely spare some." She grinned. "Did you know you can even eat the rinds on those? They're so good."

"I've never had one before. I think I'd like to try them, if you really don't mind."

"Pick as many as you want."

Mom hesitated. "I don't really know what to look for, as far as ripeness and size and whatnot."

Delia gave up on the stubborn weed and went over to look for the perfect squashes to send home with her. "You want a strong yellow with green stripes. And GeeGee said it should feel heavier than it looks, so you kinda have to pick them up and feel the heft." She chose a couple and cut them off the vine. "Here, see how these feel."

"Oh." Mom sounded surprised and bounced them in her hands a little. "Oh, I see what you mean now. Okay, honey. Go on back to what you were doing. Do you mind if I take an acorn squash or two?"

"Not at all. The more, the merrier."

"Thank you, dear."

Smiling and feeling like she'd done something good when all she'd really done was profit off GeeGee's green thumb, Delia went back to the pumpkin patch. They'd brought two baskets this time so they could each tote one, and they were well on their way to filling up both with a huge bounty. Delia figured she might as well clear out as much as possible while she had help for the canning. Less to do by herself later that way.

As she was digging some red potatoes, her phone buzzed in her pocket, and she felt dread suffuse her. Was it her stalker? Did she dare to look, or should she wait until later so she didn't worry her mother? Would she have to call the cops *again*?

Reluctantly, she stood up and pulled off her dirt-caked gloves, then pulled out her phone and tapped it on. Relief filled her when she realized it was Julie, not Creepy the Stalker Man.

> I didn't want to call while your mom was there, but how are you doing? Are things still happening? Do I need to buy a ticket and head that way?

SMILING, SHE TAPPED OUT A RESPONSE.

> I'm fine. Stuff is still happening. I'll fill you in when Mom leaves. Okay to call after, say, 7?

. . .

She waited, giving Mom a little wave when she looked over curiously. Soon enough, her phone buzzed again.

> After 7 is fine. I'm serious about buying a ticket. I don't like all this stalker-breaking-into-your-house crap.

Delia sighed and typed in a quick "Me, neither", then shoved her phone back in her pocket and went back to work.

When both baskets were overfull, they hefted them over their arms and took their tools and gloves back to the shed, then hefted the haul into the house through the back door. Delia had left it open, figuring neither of them would have a free hand to unlock the door on the way back in. Also, the door was in full view of the garden the whole time, so surely no one would be able to sneak in with both of them out there watching.

Surely not.

But she found herself feeling antsy and looking for things out of place when she walked back inside, unsettled and hating the feeling. Mom thankfully didn't seem to notice her twitchiness and went straight for the kitchen island, dropping the basket on it with a hefty grunt.

Delia added hers, then rubbed at her arm where the basket's handle had dug in. She hoped Mom's arm didn't bruise from the pressure. Her skin was getting more and more delicate as she aged.

"Well, that's quite the haul," Mom said, hands on her hips. "We'll have our work cut out for us, won't we?"

"We don't have to if you don't feel up to it." She put a hand on her mother's shoulder. "I can figure it out myself if it's too much to do."

"Nonsense," Mom said bluntly, pushing up her sleeves. "I think I can handle more than a little canning in my advanced years."

Blushing, Delia started to apologize, but Mom waved her off with a chuckle.

"I know, I know. You young people think your parents have one foot in the grave, but I'll tell you, little miss, that I still walk two miles every day. I think I can handle it."

Since that was two miles more than Delia walked in a day, she zipped her lips and went to the counter where GeeGee kept the pressure cooker during canning season. The rest of the year, it went in the pantry on a very high shelf.

"Okay, what's first?"

Mom smiled brightly. "First, we clean everything. Very, very clean. You don't want to get botulism."

Delia blanched. "No. No, I do not."

"So let's get cleaning."

So cleaning, they did.

31

Delia was sadder to see her mother driving down the driveway than she expected to be. They'd had such a lovely morning and early afternoon, even with the hot, sweaty work of canning. They talked freely about things they hadn't discussed in years. Mom even laughed at a story about one of GeeGee's séances, which surprised Delia to no end. She used to be so set against them, after all. Wouldn't even hear about that whole aspect of Delia's cherished summers.

It felt like, for the first time since she'd picked up that damn diary, she could mourn the GeeGee she used to know, all while carrying on a tradition of hers by storing up all the veggies of the harvest. It felt... good. Pure and clean.

Unfortunately, she had to admit that part of her sadness at seeing her mother go was that she was, once again, alone in a house that no longer felt entirely safe, thanks to a certain asshole stalker. Where would he pop up next? What new tricks would he try?

More importantly, would the police get here in time?

At least Luke had stopped texting her. She must have

blocked his last available number. It was, frankly, a relief. Maybe he'd given up and gone home.

Or maybe he'd followed her to a Chinese restaurant and left a message on her truck.

Suddenly aggravated, not mad or even scared but *annoyed*, she went back inside and locked the door behind her with a vicious twist of her hand. She hated feeling this way. She hated that all this shit was happening all at once, to the point where they'd all become twisted up in her mind and emotions. Grief at her stunning loss, elation and uneasiness at suddenly being wealthy, shock about the serial killer thing, fear of and annoyance at the stalker. It all swirled around her like an emotional tornado until she couldn't decide which she was feeling at any given moment.

And she was tired. So, so tired.

Dragging her feet, she went into the kitchen and made herself a pot of tea. She'd done well to stay out of GeeGee's bedroom during her mother's short stay, but she could already feel herself bracing for the revelations to come in 1982. She didn't want to know, but she needed to know. And GeeGee wanted her to read the whole thing, to try and understand. She wasn't sure she wanted to understand, but… she had to read more. She had to read them all.

So, stalker or no stalker, GeeGee's bedroom beckoned, and Delia answered its siren call. She took in her pot of tea, placed it carefully on the little table beside the chair, and went to the closet. Pushed back the dresses, where a mauve one with tiny Sakura blossoms dotting all over caught her eye, and she decided she might wear that one tomorrow, in honor of her mother's taste in colors. Opened the trunk. Dug out 1982. Went to the wingback.

Opened the cover.

I started the new year with a bang. Or, should I say, a kill.

DELIA SIGHED. THIS WASN'T GOING TO GO WELL AT ALL. SHE could already tell.

Some lovely friends invited me to a masquerade ball to ring in the new year, and I couldn't resist going. I so rarely have a chance to throw myself into colorful costumes. Maybe I should start celebrating Halloween again, like I did as a child. Why should only children be allowed to dress up in costumes and trick or treat?

I declare it now: when my house is finished, I will dress up as a witch every year for Halloween and scare the bejeesus out of all the children who come for candy.

DESPITE THE UNPLEASANT BLUNTNESS OF THE OPENING SENTENCE, Delia found herself reluctantly grinning. GeeGee had, indeed, scared the bejeesus out of plenty of kids in her day. Oh, how she'd loved putting together a different witch costume every year.

Oh, GeeGee.

Anyway, I made my masquerade costume myself, with a little help from a friend with a boutique in town. Three years ago, I read tarot for her and predicted she would meet a handsome plumber and have a nice, pleasant, middle-class life with two kids and a dog. Within six months, she met a plumber—I won't say he's handsome, but to each their own—and she already has one kid and a dog, so she felt she owed me a favor. Who am I to turn down help?

> So my costume was lovely, and I even had her sew in pockets so I could carry around one of my syringes without having to keep track of a purse at a party. People have asked me about my syringes, of course. I can't tell you how many people think I'm a diabetic. It's a wonderful excuse, and people think I want to keep it quiet, so they don't talk to each other about it. It's perfect.

AND JUST LIKE THAT, THE DEVIOUSNESS SENT A CHILL UP DELIA'S spine. She didn't know how many more swoops of emotion she could take. Not that it stopped her from reading further.

> A masquerade is like a buffet for someone like me. There's a certain amount of anonymity from the masks, and freedom to trade partners or drink more than you normally would or even try the drugs served in the back rooms of the party house. I saw cocaine, LSD, and heroin, and I wasn't even looking for that sort of good time. I didn't want to dull my senses.
> I didn't want to ruin the hunt.
> It didn't take long to find a target, either. He made his way through the crowd, grabbing ladies' asses or groping their breasts, laughing all the while like it was great fun. He got slapped at least three times, just since I started watching him, the bastard.
> I hate men like him. They think women are objects for them to nuzzle and squeeze, like fruit at a market. Well, he found out that prickly things lurk in the market stalls.
> A heart attack, the paper said the next day. Too much cocaine. They found him in a broom closet with his pantaloons open and his dick in his hand.
> I thought that was a nice touch. He deserved to be remembered as the hanging-out prick that he was.
> Happy New Year to me.

. . .

Shuddering, Delia turned the page and read on to the next entry, reaching for her tea. She hadn't expected to read about an actual murder, somehow. All the prior entries had been about murders past, about GeeGee trying to understand her own nature. Delia hadn't expected....

But she should have. She should have known that, with all the years between the 1980s and now, at least one murder would be cataloged, dissected, and discussed.

Swallowing grimly, she read on.

I went to the old spot today. I told the contractor that I wanted to get a feel for the house's progress, but I really wanted to go back to where it all began. My first kill.

Delia slammed the book closed, not bothering to mark the page.

No. No, she wouldn't believe it. It couldn't be.

GeeGee did not build The Hollows on the grave of her first kill. Please, god, don't let it be. Delia couldn't bear thinking about living on top of a burial mound.

It took all her willpower to not throw the book at the wall. She paced back and forth in the room, her thoughts racing. How could GeeGee do that? How could she memorialize her first murder by building her goddamned house on the property she'd killed someone on? What kind of psychopath—

But that was just it. GeeGee *was* a psychopath. It was all over the pages of her diary, leaking through all her passages about not being sure she knew what love was, not connecting with anyone, not having any human restraint or real regret about her crimes—in fact, having regret over *not* regretting her crimes.

GeeGee was a psychopath, or a sociopath. Honestly, Delia forgot which was which. Either way, it meant that her beloved great grandaunt, the woman who had nurtured her at least as much if not more than her own mother, the woman who had left her a fortune and claimed to love her... was incapable of actual love.

A pain so swift and sudden that it felt like a knife thrust sliced through her, and she was on her knees on the floor of GeeGee's room before she could stop herself. Sobs wracked her frame, and she pressed her hands to her face in a futile attempt to stem the flood. The gesture was about as effective as that old king who supposedly tried to command the tide, though. The tears just kept coming.

Tears of grief. Tears of betrayal. Tears of rage. Yes, suddenly she was so full of rage that if her stalker stood before her, she thought she might beat him to a bloody pulp.

Why did GeeGee have to write all this shit down? Why couldn't she just keep it to herself? Why couldn't Delia have her awesome, glowing memories of all the time they spent together safe in her heart forever? Why did she have to lose those good times, now that they were all tainted by madness?

Why was all of this happening? When would it just fucking *stop?*

Glass shattered somewhere in the house.

Delia gasped, her sobs cutting off mid-weep. Another clash of broken glass and the tinkle of it hitting the hardwood floor sent another gasp tearing through her. Someone was breaking in. Her stalker, brazen asshole that he was, was literally breaking into her house.

Hands shaking, she swiped at her tears with one hand and pulled out her phone with the other. She hit the emergency button and waited for it to connect.

"911, what's the address of your emergency?"

"The Hollows out on Old 66. Someone just broke the glass in my front door. I have a stalker, and I think he's literally breaking in. Please send Officer Jenkins or Officer Taliferro out right now. They know the situation."

"Is this Miss Jameson?"

"Yes, this is Delia Jameson. Please hurry!"

"I have three units dispatched out your way, Miss Jameson. Is there some place safe you can hide until they get there?"

But at the word "hide", Delia felt her back stiffening. She didn't want to hide. She didn't want this asshole to have that much power over her. In fact, right now, she was so full of roiling emotion that she felt like she could take on a whole troop of stalkers.

"Just hurry, please."

"Ma'am, don't hang up—"

Delia hung up. Then, she stood up and squared her shoulders.

It was time to take out the goddamn trash.

32

Delia took off her shoes before doing anything else. Socked feet would be quieter than even her soft-soled tennis shoes, and she wanted stealth right now, not surety of step. She might step on some broken glass, but that was a chance she was willing to take.

Once she was sock-footed, she crept out of GeeGee's bedroom and into the hallway, sticking as close to the wall as possible without rubbing against it. If stairs were less likely to creak on either side, surely the hallway would be the same.

She heard someone rummaging around in the drawers of the credenza in the foyer and quickly tiptoed to the other side of the hall. She wanted the element of surprise, and she risked being seen if she stayed on the other side. This way, she'd pop out practically right beside him.

For a moment, she paused, wishing she had a weapon. Then, she heard a low curse and clomping footsteps moving over toward the parlor. She didn't want him in there. That was GeeGee's favorite room. Right now, that seemed like the only important consideration.

Gathering her courage and strength, she hurried up the

hallway to where it joined the foyer and peered out into the gloom. There he was, back to her, one hand shining a flashlight into the parlor. Looking for her? Well, he'd by god found her.

Moving quickly and lightly, she ran across the parlor and launched herself onto his back, grabbing on with both arms and legs. He shouted in surprise and flung back the flashlight. It slammed into her head at the temple, but she just shouted in pain and held on tighter, trying to throw him off-balance and wrestle him to the floor. He was strong, though. Hideously strong.

Instead of going down, he reached back with his other hand and grabbed a fistful of hair, yanking hard enough that he almost ripped it right out of her scalp. She screamed and lifted herself up, practically crawling up over his shoulder to bite him on the neck. He shouted and pulled his hand loose, tearing out a few strands of hair. Then, he shoved at her face, dropping the flashlight to grab onto one of her legs wrapped around him and pry at it.

"Get off me, you crazy bitch!"

Crazy bitch, huh? He hadn't seen crazy yet. Gritting her teeth, she held on around his neck with one arm and used the other hand to claw at his face, digging in her short nails. He shouted again and spun around, almost dislodging her with the sudden movement. Her head spun, but she hung on even as blood trickled into her eye from where he'd bashed her with the flashlight.

"Jesus Christ, lady!"

She grabbed a fistful of stocking cap and yanked it off, then grabbed a handful of hair and yanked sideways, again trying to knock him off his balance. She'd have better leverage if they were both on the ground. He was too much bigger than her standing up. She didn't stand a chance like this.

She heard a car racing up the driveway, engine roaring, and let out a triumphant shout. She'd never know how the police got here so fast, but she didn't care. She would kiss whoever broke down her front door right about now.

"Shit!"

She bit him again, yanking his hair with the other hand, and he stumbled around in a circle, trying to dislodge her. She held on as tight as she could, hoping she was choking him with her arm around his neck. The bastard. How dare he break into her house. How dare he torment her and scare her and make her afraid to be alone.

"Delia!"

She recognized that voice, but it wasn't one of the cops. She was so surprised, in fact, that she almost let go and slipped down the stalker's back a little. He dialed up his thrashing, too, which didn't help her hold on.

Someone kicked the door in just as her grip slipped entirely and she went flying to the floor in the middle of the room.

"Delia, honey, are you—you bastard!"

Luke. It was Luke launching himself across her parlor to tangle with her stalker intruder. How could that be? Luke *was* her stalker... wasn't he?

Head spinning, she pushed up to her elbows to watch the two men punching each other in her foyer, bashing into the walls and knocking things off to crash to the floor. It was a goddamn melee, and she was too woozy to tell who was winning. Then, the intruder shoved Luke away enough to bend down and pick up the flashlight.

"Luke, look out!"

The lens broke as it cracked down on the back of Luke's head, the light going out like a snuffed candle. Luke went down. The intruder broke away and ran out the door just as more cars came roaring up the drive, strobes painting the night in flashes of red and blue.

"Goddammit!"

The first car crunched to a halt, slinging gravel, and a car door opened even before it could possibly be in park.

"Freeze, asshole!"

The intruder growled and threw up his hands, a black cutout in the kaleidoscope of lights flaring through the open door. Delia let herself fall back to the hardwood floor, then groggily pushed back up.

"Luke? Luke, are you—?"

"I'm alive. Ow, shit." He grunted. "How about you? Are you okay?"

"I dunno."

Policemen surged up onto her porch, taking the intruder into custody. It had to be Eli, and she couldn't even begin to think what would happen to him now. His reputation would be in the shitter once he went to jail for breaking and entering, assault, and who knew what other charges.

She swallowed hard and slumped back to the floor, blood gumming in her eye, her head aching.

Oh, Elijah, she thought, wanting to cry all over again. What have you done?

33

Head aching, Delia fought not to touch the patch of gauze taped to her temple. She didn't need stitches, the EMT said, but the flashlight had broken the skin. She would probably have a scar. Her forehead would match her knees, she thought, then closed her eyes against a rush of regret.

Elijah. How could he? And why?

She looked over at Luke. What an unlikely hero. And yet, he'd saved her, and to his detriment. The flashlight had opened a goose egg on the crown of his head, and an EMT was butterfly-bandaging his head shut.

"Miss Jameson?"

She jerked her attention away from Luke and immediately regretted it as her head swam. She again closed her eyes.

"You okay, there?"

"Yeah, sorry. Just… moved too fast." She opened her eyes. "Go ahead, Officer Jenkins."

"Right. Okay." He shuffled his feet in the gravel, looking at the notebook in his hand. "He wasn't carrying any ID and refuses to talk, but we'll figure him out soon enough."

"I don't need to know."

Luke looked at her strangely, likely curious about her sorry tone, but didn't interrupt. Bless him. Jenkins just looked up from his notebook.

"I just need to know that it'll stop now."

Jenkins nodded. "It should. We have him in custody. Good thing your friend got here when he did."

"Yes," she said, looking at Luke with grateful eyes. "A very good thing."

Luke smiled softly.

"You're done, Mr. Sullivan." The EMT wadded up packaging and tossed it into the back of the ambulance. "Don't scratch while it's healing. If you have any infection, there's a clinic in town."

"Okay, thanks."

Delia frowned a little, wincing at the pain in her temple as her face moved. He wouldn't still be here to visit a clinic. Surely he had a job to get back to. He couldn't just camp out in Missouri forever, waiting for her to change her mind.

She was grateful for the rescue, but a shot to the head hadn't ruined her memory of what he'd done to her in California.

The EMTs started packing up their ambulance, so she scooted off Lola's bumper and stood on her own two shaky feet. She was fine, she reminded herself. She had a good, hard head. It was just a reaction to all the violence kicking in.

"You okay, there, Miss Jameson?" Officer Jenkins sounded surprisingly fretful. "Do you need me to help you back into the house?"

She smiled crookedly, trying not to engage the injured side of her head. "No thanks, Officer Jenkins. I'm just a little wobbly. I'll be fine."

"I'll help," Luke said, shuffling over from where the EMTs were slamming the ambulance doors shut and getting ready to leave. "I think we should all sit down for a minute and gather our thoughts."

Delia's phone chimed, and she cursed under her breath. What a time for a phone call. How would she even begin to explain what had just happened?

But it was Mr. Langston, not Mom or Julie. What on earth?

"Hello? Mr. Langston?" She walked a little away from the men. "Is everything okay?"

"I should be asking you that, Miss Delia. Are you alright? I just got word that there was a fracas at your house tonight."

She blinked. "How…?"

"My paralegal has a police band radio."

"Jesus, does everyone have one of those around here?"

"Just about." He sounded briefly amused, but when he spoke again, he was deadly serious. "But seriously, Miss Delia, are you alright?"

"I'm okay." She huffed. "Took a shot to the head, and a friend of mine also got one, but we're both fine, considering. Elijah Campbell broke into my house, and I fought back, is all."

"Elijah Campbell? Do you mean Eli?" He sounded gobsmacked. "The accountant? That hardly tracks, Miss Delia."

"I know, but my stalker had to be either Luke or Eli, and Luke broke in to rescue me. It had to be Eli."

"Why does it have to be one of those two?"

"Because they're the only ones who knew I was back and that I'd inherited. Why else would anyone want to stalk me?"

"I suppose." But he didn't sound convinced. "I'll admit that he's called Barrett Davidson's office multiple times this past week, lobbying for his firm to be appointed your local accountants, but that's a far cry from tormenting and stalking you. Breaking into your house and assaulting you."

The last piece of the puzzle clicked into place, and she shut her eyes. Oh, Elijah. You could've just asked.

Out loud, she said, "It was him, Mr. Langston. But that's good because that means it's over. The stalker is arrested. I'm safe now."

"Well, that is a relief, anyway." He still sounded unconvinced, but his tone warmed. "I'm just glad to know you're alright. I'll call again to check on you in a day or two."

"Okay. Thank you, Mr. Langston."

"Goodnight, Miss Delia."

"Goodnight."

She tapped the End button and shoved her phone into her pocket, then turned back to Officer Jenkins, only to find Luke practically standing on top of her. She startled, jerking back, and he reached out and caught her before she could stumble. His hands were gentle, but the sudden move scared her, just the same.

Just her adrenaline still jumping, she thought.

"You okay? Who was that?"

"My lawyer." She grinned wryly. "Apparently everybody has a police band radio in this town."

Luke's eyebrows rose. "Your lawyer is still on duty at eight o'clock on a Sunday night?"

She huffed. "Apparently, when you're rich, your lawyer is on duty twenty-four seven."

His eyebrows rose further, and he stepped back a step. "You're rich?"

She winced, wanting to kick herself. She was so off her game at the moment. She didn't mean to blurt that out. She didn't mean to confirm his assumption.

"Well, I got the house, anyway." She shrugged, like it was no big deal. "GeeGee didn't want it sold off to some stranger."

That was the truth, at least. God forbid someone should go digging around and find a goddamn skeleton. Surely, there was just the one. Don't shit where you eat, right? GeeGee wouldn't have squirreled away more bodies on her home property, would she?

She shook herself. "Look, Luke. I really appreciate the help, but I could stand to get to bed early. It's been a rough few days, and I'm really tired." A sudden thought occurred to her, and she tilted her head to one side. "Wait, why are you here, anyway?"

He looked down at his feet, which shuffled back and forth in the gravel. "You blocked all my numbers, and I really wanted to talk to you. I know I shouldn't have shown up without warning again, but... I couldn't give you any notice."

She rolled her eyes. Of course he would push his luck. Of course he would show up at the house, yet again, and bull his way into her life, one way or another. That's just who he was, rescue aside.

But that was a conversation for another time. She really was tired, and she thought she'd be able to sleep tonight, what with her stalker locked up in a jail cell.

"I can see you're tired," Luke said, reaching out to lightly touch her upper arm. "We'll talk tomorrow, okay?"

If we must, she thought but didn't say. Instead, she just nodded and went over to say goodnight to Officer Jenkins, who was still waiting for her, though the rest of the cops must have left while she was talking to Mr. Langston.

"Everything okay, Miss Delia?"

She nodded wearily. "I'm fine. Just tired."

"Adrenaline rush wearing off," he said, nodding sagely. "You'll sleep like the dead tonight, I'll bet."

She grinned crookedly to save her poor head. "Is there anything else I need to do? I could really stand a hot bath and an ice pack before I go to bed."

"No, Miss Delia, I think you've had enough excitement for one night. You get some sleep, and we'll be in touch when we get your stalker processed. I'll keep you notified of how his case is proceeding. And I guess we don't have to go looking into your ex-boyfriend anymore, so there's that."

"Good." She hadn't thought of that, but it tracked. "Thank you, Officer Jenkins."

"Goodnight, Miss Delia. Get some rest."

"Goodnight."

Luke's car, likely a rental, drove off into the night, followed by Jenkins' cruiser. Just like that, Delia was alone. She shuffled up the steps and inside the house, then just stood in the foyer, looking around. The credenza drawers were all pulled out, the stuff inside rifled through. Pictures had been knocked off the walls during the struggle. There was broken glass all over the floor, making her glad she'd put on her shoes after the cops arrived.

Tomorrow, she told herself. She would clean it all up tomorrow.

So, exhausted and heartsore at the thought of her old childhood friend betraying her so fully, she shuffled up the stairs to her room. She wanted a hot bath. She wanted a pile of blankets.

And good god, she wanted some sleep.

34

Delia woke up with a headache fit to burn the house down. She forgot to take any pain relievers before going to bed, and she slept like the dead, just as Officer Jenkins predicted. She needed Tylenol, stat.

Groaning, she rolled over and reached for her phone. Jesus, it was almost ten o'clock. She really had slept like the dead. She yawned and stretched, her head pounding sickly, then rolled out of bed with a hand to the gauze patch on her temple. It was still in place and didn't feel wet, so maybe she hadn't bled through. There was no blood on her pillow, so that was good.

She needed to call her mom and tell her everything that had happened. She needed to text Julie to see if she was up. She needed to call Officer Jenkins to see if she should be doing anything.

But she really, really needed some Tylenol first. Her head was killing her.

She dragged her feet all the way to the bathroom, then winced as she turned on the light. Too bright, but she needed to see what she was taking. GeeGee had filled her medicine cabinet with supplements of all sorts. All natural, of course. The

Tylenol was Delia's. GeeGee had sniffed at the sight of it but never removed it.

Of course, it was at least five years old, but surely it would still work enough to give her some relief. She'd experiment with peppermint essential oil and mugwort and the like when the pain stopped throbbing.

When she'd taken the maximum dosage of Tylenol and relieved herself and brushed her teeth, she wrapped up in her kimono and went downstairs for the mauve dress with the Sakura blossoms. She wanted comfort today, even if that meant wearing GeeGee's serial killer clothes. She wanted a flowy dress, and she wanted a cardigan. She even wanted a pair of GeeGee's comfortable flats, if they would fit. She'd never tried on GeeGee's shoes before, but they were a similar size in everything else now, so it couldn't hurt to try.

The dress fit like a dream with its peasant blouse-like neckline and sleeves and its flowing skirt. The material was a little thin for the chill in the air, but Delia had planned on wearing a cardigan, anyway. She knew just the one, too—one GeeGee had crocheted herself in shades of green. It, of course, had pockets. So did the dress.

And the shoes fit just about right. They were a little wide, but not enough that she worried about stepping out of them by accident. They looked like they were crocheted, like the cardigan, but they were in a neutral shade of taupe that matched anything. She felt positively swathed in comfort, which was exactly what she needed today.

Thinking about breakfast, wondering if it was too soon for the famous poached egg, mascarpone, avocado, and English muffin sandwiches to make a comeback, she went out into the foyer and its wall of cardigans. Just as she chose the green crocheted one, she heard the porch swing chains creak and froze, all her fears coming back to her.

He was still locked up, wasn't he? Wouldn't Officer Jenkins

have called if they'd let him out? Jesus, was she still safe, or had it all been some sort of cruel illusion?

The chains creaked again, and she felt a tired sort of resolve fill her. She squared her shoulders and went to the door, unlocking it and throwing it open in one quick move. In a flash, she stood on the porch with her fists up, ready to fight.

Luke jerked up off the swing with his hands up to show he was innocent.

"Whoa, there, tiger." He huffed a nervous laugh. "It's just me. Sorry, did I wake you? I was trying to let you sleep."

Her jaw tightened. "Luke? What the hell are you doing here?"

"We said we'd talk tomorrow. It's tomorrow. I still can't text or call you, remember?"

Her breath fell out of her, and she suddenly felt weak. "Jesus, Luke, you scared the shit out of me. Why are you here so early?"

"It's practically lunch time."

She looked at her phone. "It's 10:42. That is not practically lunch time. How long have you been here?"

He looked sheepish. "Uh. Since nine?"

She closed her eyes and let her head fall back. It already ached again, and she couldn't take any more Tylenol for four hours.

"Sorry, Delia. I just really wanted to talk to you."

I didn't want to talk to you. But she didn't say that out loud. He had saved her last night, no matter how selfish he was being today. Sighing, she gestured for him to follow her inside. She stopped for the chosen cardigan, though, and shrugged into it before leading the way to the kitchen.

"This is a great place," he said, looking around as he followed her. "Lots of character."

"Lots of glass on the floor." She sighed again. "Do you want breakfast? I was just going to make something."

"I could definitely eat."

She wanted to roll her eyes, but she restrained herself. It

would only hurt her poor head. Instead, she went to the fridge for eggs, then squeeze-checked the avocados to make sure they were still good. They had the maddening tendency to go from rock-hard to rotten in no time flat. Thankfully, these were still good.

Luke was mercifully quiet as she poached the eggs, peeled and sliced the avocados, and toasted the English muffins. He didn't offer to help, but he would've just been in her way, anyway. Better to have him leaning on the other side of the kitchen island.

"What's all this stuff?"

She glanced back to see him inspecting all the canning she and her mother had done the day before. Jesus, was that just yesterday?

"Canned vegetables. I haven't had time to take them down to the cellar yet."

"Oh. You can vegetables? Since when?"

"Since I have a garden."

"Oh."

He was quiet for a minute, but she could practically feel him searching for another conversational gambit. He wasn't the type of man who could stay quiet for long. It was one of his least endearing traits. Like the cheating.

"So how are you doing, Delia? Really?"

She sighed. "I'm fine, Luke. It's just been a big week. That's all."

"Seriously, DD. This is me you're talking to. I know you're not okay about GeeGee or the break-in or any of this. You can talk to me, you know. I still love you."

She slumped. "Luke, let's get something straight from the start." She turned away from the half-built sandwiches and stared him in the eyes. "We are not together. We will never again be together. You cheated on me. You broke my heart. I will never allow that again. Period."

"DD—"

"And don't call me that. I'm not a pair of breasts."

"What?" He looked comically confused. "That's not—" He shook his head. "Okay, Delia. I won't. But if you could just give me another chance—"

"Luke, stop." She put up both hands, as if the physical gesture would help stop him. "It's not gonna happen. Let it go. I appreciate your help last night, thank you very much, but it's over. It will always be over."

"Delia—"

Her phone chimed. Groaning, she pulled it out of her cardigan pocket only to squint down at the number. It looked vaguely familiar, but she didn't recognize it. She held up one finger as Luke started to speak, then swiped to answer.

"Hello?"

"Delia?"

She almost dropped the phone. Elijah. Elijah was on her phone. Was he out? Surely he wouldn't spend his one phone call to call her, would he? Or was the one phone call thing just a TV-land fallacy?

"Elijah," she breathed, her knees weak. She turned away from Luke's suddenly thunderous expression. "Jesus Christ."

"Why the hell is your lawyer calling my boss to ask why I'm in jail?"

Her mouth worked, but no sound came out.

"Delia? Seriously, what the hell? I knew you didn't want to talk to me, but telling everyone I'm in prison? Why would you do that? I'm at work right now, and everyone's staring at me like I'm a criminal!"

He was at work? How was that possible? He was supposed to be in jail. It was supposed to be *over*.

"Elijah…." It was breathy, but it was at least a word. "I thought they locked you up."

"But why? Why on earth would you think that?"

"But if it wasn't you—"

She felt a sharp pain in the side of her neck, followed by a wave of heat. She felt immediately woozy, and as she faded, she wondered if this was what all of GeeGee's victims felt like as they died of an air embolism. Because that was a needle in her neck.

And all was going dark.

"Delia?"

That voice was far and wee, fading into the black.

"Delia, answer me—"

And then, it was gone.

35

It hurt to wake up. Delia moaned softly, her head—hell, her whole body aching. She tried to raise a hand to her aching head, but she couldn't. She was... her hands were tied. To a chair? Where the hell was she?

"Okay, so things may have gotten a little out of hand."

She blinked groggy eyes, squinting in the bright light of... the parlor? Yes. She was tied to one of the spindly, fancy, velvet-cushioned chairs in the parlor. And there stood Luke, looking for all the world like a chastened little boy instead of like the man who had just drugged her with god knows what.

"But you just wouldn't listen, DD. You never listened to me. I tried to explain that I'm a man, and I have needs, but no. You locked up like a safety deposit box in a bank and wouldn't let me in."

"So you drugged me?" she demanded, twisting her wrists to see how tightly she was tied up.

Not good. Too tight to wriggle her hands loose without losing some skin. Then, very slowly because she was still drugged, the light dawned.

"It was you the whole time. That's why Elijah isn't in jail, because it's you. What... did you hire someone to break in and jump me? Who the hell was that guy?"

"Hey, now. There wasn't supposed to be any jumping. I don't know how that happened. He was just supposed to scare you, and then I'd scare him off, and you'd be grateful and take me back. That's it."

"That's it? That's *it?*" She felt herself practically screeching and wanted to stop, but her body wouldn't listen to her. "He could've killed me! He could've killed you!"

"Not if he wanted to get paid." He muttered under his breath. "And he's sure as hell not getting paid now."

She wanted to clap her hands to her head. She didn't understand. Why on earth would he do this? Why would he stalk her and break into her house and scare the living shit out of her?

Frankly, those were excellent questions to ask out loud.

"Why, Luke? Why would you do this?"

"Because I need the money, goddammit!" He paced back and forth, running his hands through his hair until it stuck up in corkscrews. "I haven't worked in months, and I owe people. California is fucking expensive, okay? You know that. You know how it is. I thought if we could just get married now that you're rolling in it—"

"How did you know?"

"—everything would—what? Know what?"

She suddenly felt very small and still. "That GeeGee died. That I was inheriting everything. It wasn't the internet, was it? Someone told you."

He waved this away. "Julie told me. That's not important. I need to figure out how to—"

"Julie?" She felt even more still. "Why would Julie tell you any of that?"

"Because we're fucking. Focus, DD. We're gonna fix this."

But she was overwhelmed by a roaring in her ears. Not Julie.

Not her only real friend since all of their mutual friends deserted her after he dumped her. Not her Julie.

"Here's what we're gonna do. You are going to give me... a half million. You can afford that. You always said your GeeGee had big bucks, so you can afford that much, easy. You give me a half million, and I let you go, and I go back to California, and we go our separate ways with nobody ending up dead or in jail. Deal?"

She wanted to cry. She'd lost everyone. GeeGee was a serial killer. Luke was a cheater and her stalker. Elijah was... well, she supposed Eli was alright, but it was hard to jump from thinking he was jailed for stalking her to thinking of him as a friend. Especially since he'd likely never talk to her again after her lawyer asked his boss why he was in jail.

And now Julie—

"Delia? Do we have a deal?"

She gritted her teeth, yet again denied the chance to grieve a loss. "You're insane."

He sighed. She twisted her wrists, but the pull was too tight. She looked down at the bindings, and it looked like he'd tied her up with a phone charger cord stretched between the two chair arms. That didn't leave a lot of wiggle room. She didn't think she'd be able to get her hands free with that little distance between the arms.

"Delia, honey, I'm doing you a favor here. I could just kill you now." He pulled a small amber bottle from his pocket and shook it. "GHB. If I give you enough, you'll die."

She scoffed, though she'd suddenly gone cold right through to her core. "Then you wouldn't get any money."

"True. That's why I'm trying to work this out between us. You give me the money, and I give you your life. It didn't have to be this way, but you never could leave things alone. You never could just take me for what I am."

The chair was spindly. She'd rarely ever sat in the fancy

chairs outside of a séance because they felt fragile. Were they? Maybe now was a good time to find out.

"And what are you, Luke? A psychopath?"

She wiggled back and forth, hoping he wouldn't notice. The chair didn't creak, but it did feel like it was twisting with her movements. Good.

"A man with vision. A man who gets things done."

She snorted. "What have you gotten done, Luke? What? How'd that start-up work out for you? Or the video game—*my* video game—you wanted to develop? Or the body-building supplements? Or whatever other get-rich-quick scheme came your way." Twisting with a little more force, she laughed harshly. "You're not a man with vision. You're a loser. You've always been a loser. You'll always be a loser."

"Wait right there."

The venom in his voice made her want to shrink back into the chair, but he actually left the room, which gave her the opportunity she needed. She started rocking the chair back and forth on the thick rug GeeGee had put under the séance table so no one would accuse her of tapping her feet on the hardwoods. It muffled the sound of her rocking, but then the chair squealed, nails pulling against the wood. Almost there.

"What the hell are you—"

The chair fell over on its side, one arm breaking loose as it cracked against the floor. Delia's elbow hit, too, and sent a shock up to her shoulder, but she shrugged it off. Twisting her wrists, she managed to pull one of her hands free of the loosened power cord.

"Jesus, Delia, can't you just sit fucking still!"

He lunged at her, and she realized he had the empty syringe in his hand. He'd gone to the kitchen for it. Jesus, he really was going to shoot her up with GHB, not that she really knew what that was outside of a party drug. She didn't want to take her chances, though, and doubled her efforts to get her other hand loose and kick free of the remains of the chair.

Her hand finally came untangled, minus a little skin, and she reached up just as he threw himself down on her. The air blasted out of her with the force of the hit, but she swung one hand and knocked the syringe out of his grip. It skittered across the hardwood floor, out of the fight. Neither of them could reach it now.

"Goddammit, Delia!"

Growling, he clamped his hands on her neck before she could stop him.

"Can't you just fucking do one fucking thing I say? Just for once? You stupid, annoying, pain in the ass *bitch!*"

She choked, trying to scream without any air, clawing at his hands, his arms, even his face. He squeezed his hands harder. She socked the heel of her hand under his chin, pushing him away with one hand, reaching futilely toward the syringe with the other. It was out of reach, but she was desperate. So desperate.

Dying. She was dying. Her head felt like it was about to explode, her throat on fire, her lungs heaving for air that wouldn't come.

Suddenly, the syringe was in her reaching hand. Not questioning her luck, she closed her hand around it in a fist. She raised it up over his neck and slammed the needle home at the base of his skull, right where GeeGee used to. She pushed the plunger down.

Luke stopped. His expression went... curious, then blank. His hands loosened, fell away, and she sucked in a huge, tearing breath. He fell over her, dead weight pressing her into the floor, silent now even as his weight drove the fresh air right out of her lungs.

Scrambling and gasping, she shoved at his body until she rolled him enough to scoot half out from under him, then collapsed. Her lungs were on fire, her throat lined with sandpaper. But she was breathing, and that was a damn sight better than two seconds ago.

Then, like music to her ears, she heard sirens in the distance.

Closing her eyes, Delia lay on the floor half under her dead ex-boyfriend and waited for the cavalry to arrive.

36

Officer Jenkins laid a copied piece of paper on the little table in the window nook. It was a black and white mugshot of a teenager with a mohawk and a goatee. Delia recognized Luke anyway and sucked in a deep breath.

"Luke Sullivan, twenty years ago. I'm so sorry, Miss Delia. It took a while for us to get his juvenile record because it was sealed. We only got it this morning, and... well, I'd already stopped looking at him."

She swallowed painfully, her freezing hands locked around a cup of hot honey lemon tea. It was supposed to soothe her throat. She didn't know if it was working yet or not.

"What did he do?"

"Petty theft, breaking and entering—probably how he was able to get in even though your doors and windows were locked —minor assault charges, you name it. He was a busy little bee until he hit eighteen and realized he'd be doing grown-up time in grown-up prison if he didn't clean up his act."

She would sigh if she didn't know it would hurt. "I just thought he was a loser. Not an actual criminal."

"I think it's safe to say he was both, Miss Delia." He sighed.

"We figure he was squatting over at old Miss Gladys' house so he could be close enough to watch you. Your neighbor, Mr. Don Brinkley, reported a strange car pulling out of the driveway yesterday evening, but we never connected it. I'm so sorry we didn't."

She breathed deeply, then winced and sipped her tea. Luke had been literally next door, though there was some distance between the houses, and she'd never even guessed. She would sigh, but her throat hurt too much.

"What about the thug? The one he hired to break in for real?"

"Just a local tough. He's not talking, though. He's already lawyered up." He shrugged. "He also has a record, but a much more recent one. He's a frequent flier."

She nodded slowly. It was all too much. At this point, she just wanted her mother—who, she was glad to know, was on her way. She hoped Mom drove safely. Delia couldn't afford to lose anyone else.

"I just have one question for you, Miss Delia."

Wearily, she looked at him. "Shoot."

"How did you know to inject him with air?"

She felt her face freeze over and hoped he didn't notice. She couldn't tell him about the diaries now. Not when she'd killed someone just like GeeGee had. Jesus, wouldn't that be a doozy to explain?

"I didn't. I thought he'd already loaded it with GHB."

"Ah. Well, it's a good thing you did what you did. You'll be wearing those finger marks for a while, but it's better than the alternative."

The EMTs—the same ones who'd patched her head just last night—had given her chemical ice packs to hopefully keep down the swelling, but her throat felt puffy anyway. And bruised. She felt like she'd been through a war.

Then again, she supposed she had. There had even been a

casualty.

"Look, Miss Delia, I hate to leave you alone right now. When did you say your mother would be here again?"

"Don't worry about me, Officer Jenkins. I can take care of myself."

He looked at her with sympathy. "I don't doubt that, but are you really up to it at the moment?"

"No." She didn't shake her head. It would hurt too much. "But I'll be okay, anyway."

"Knock knock."

She shuddered, then winced at the pain singing through her body. She never wanted to hear anyone say "knock knock" ever again. Even if it was Elijah Campbell being held back in the foyer by Officer Taliferro.

"Mr. Campbell." Officer Jenkins shot her a questioning look, and she nodded as little as she thought she could get away with. "Well, you have my number, Miss Delia. You give me a call if you have any more trouble. Okay?"

"Okay. Thank you, Officer Jenkins."

"Let him in."

Taliferro reluctantly stepped aside, then followed Jenkins out of the house. She took another sip of her honey lemon tea, willing it to make her stop feeling strangled. So far, it wasn't working.

"Jesus, Delia, you look like you went ten rounds with the champ."

"Thank you, Eli. You should see the other guy."

He came over and sat down at the table, reaching out to lightly touch one of her bruised wrists. She didn't jerk away, but she didn't like the touch, either. She looked at him levelly until he stopped.

"Are you alright?"

She swallowed painfully. "No. I don't think I am."

"Oh, Delia."

He reached toward her face, and she ducked away, then made a soft little sound of pain.

"Sorry, sorry. I didn't mean to—" He cut himself off. "Sorry. I didn't think. That was stupid of me."

"Why are you here, Eli?"

"Hey," he said softly. "Don't do that. I came to check on you. Aren't we still friends?"

Again, she looked at him on the level. "Did you or did you not try to cozy up to me just to get my account for your firm?"

"What? Why would you think that?"

But he looked guilty. She knew that look. She'd seen it on Luke's face too many times to count. She was so tired of that look.

"Because my lawyer told me you've been calling my money guy, petitioning for your company to become my accounting firm."

"Delia, that's not—"

"Don't, Eli. Just don't. I'm not in the mood. I already have an accounting firm in St. Louis. You're not getting the job."

"Delia, can't we talk about this?"

"No. Maybe if you'd just asked me like a goddamn grown-up, but not now." She looked at him with the surety of a woman who knew she could kill a man if she had to. It must have worked because he recoiled. "I think you should leave, Eli. I won't be going to dinner with you again."

Without another word, without a backward glance, Elijah Campbell walked out of her life. She wasn't sorry to see him go.

Deciding she might as well do all the unpleasant things at once now that she was alone, she reluctantly picked up her phone and scrolled to Julie's number. It rang twice before she answered.

"Hey, girl. How are things going in the sticks?"

Delia didn't mince words. She didn't have the stamina for it right now.

"You were fucking Luke, and you never told me."

"What?"

She closed her eyes. "You were all I had left, Julie. Just you and Mom. How could you fuck him after everything he did to me?" Tears started in her eyes, but she refused to shed them. "Were you fucking him while we were together?"

"Delia, I wouldn't—I would *never*—"

"Just answer the question, Julie. I don't have the energy for bullshit right now."

"No." But Julie sounded angry. Angry and scared. "Delia, whatever he told you, it's bullshit—"

"No, it's not. Because how else did he learn that GeeGee had died before anyone but you and Mom knew? How else would he know when I'd be here so he could show up on my porch? And who else could tell him that I'd inherited?"

"Delia, please, it's not like that. I didn't know he'd go there. I never suspected he would stalk you and—"

"Goodbye, Julie. Don't call me again."

"Del—"

She hung up and blocked the number, then put down her phone and let the tears come. She cried for all the losses, all the things she'd never have again. She grieved.

And when she was done, she stood up, put aside her useless tea, and picked up a broom to start cleaning up. Her mother would be here in a few hours, and Delia didn't want to distress her any more than she was already likely to be distressed.

As she swept, she thought. She had killed a man today. She ought to start her own diary, like GeeGee had.

Would she start to crave it, like GeeGee? Had she not felt a rush of... *something*... when she'd seen the light go out of Luke's eyes? Was it the simple victory over someone who'd been trying to kill her, or was it something worse? Something much darker?

She swept broken glass into the dustpan, then took it to the kitchen and dumped it in the trash. Then, she went back into the foyer and picked up the broken pictures, pushed back in all the drawers in the credenza, straightened the pictures that hadn't fallen. She even went into the parlor and picked up the remains of the chair she'd broken. It didn't look destroyed beyond repair. She could probably have it fixed, since it was a matched set of six that went with the table.

Should she do séances, like GeeGee had? She knew how to cold read. She knew how to draw out the moment so someone would be compelled to answer for her.

She knew how to kill a man, too. Just another thing she couldn't unknow.

Sighing, she piled the broken chair together and decided to have someone come out and assess the damage later. See if it could be repaired. It would surely be cheaper than buying a new chair and less weird than only having five chairs at the séance table.

Then, she gave up all the subterfuge and went to GeeGee's room, where she really wanted to be. She was still in the mauve dress with Sakura blossoms, though there was now a tear under one arm, and still wearing the crocheted green cardigan. She even still had GeeGee's flats on her feet. She practically was GeeGee today.

What harm to read about more murders now that she'd committed one, even if it was to save her own life? What harm to live on ground where now two men had died, though only one had stayed? What harm to seek her future, not in tarot cards but in GeeGee's diaries?

Sighing painfully, she settled herself in the wingback chair, picked up 1982, and began to read where she left off.

I went to the old spot today. I told the contractor that I wanted to get a feel for the house's progress, but I really wanted to go back to where it all began. My first kill.

I went to the old pond and looked across the still water. He never floated up to the top to be discovered, not in all these years. Water bodies do that, I've learned. They fill up with gasses and bloat up and float to the surface. But Tommy didn't.

I stuffed him with too many rocks.

SHE CLOSED HER EYES, SWALLOWING AGAINST THE PAIN IN HER throat, and vowed to have the old pond filled in. It always scummed over with algae anyway. She thought with a shudder of all the summer days she'd spent swimming in that pond.

Suddenly, she didn't want to read any more today. She closed the book on the oracle card and put it on the end table, then just sat in the wingback, staring at nothing. Feeling nothing.

Tomorrow. Tomorrow, she'd feel. Tomorrow, she'd think. She'd think long and hard about her future.

Tomorrow, she'd try to pick herself up out of the shattered remains of her old life and start something new. Maybe she'd sit down and write out a script for that online game she'd been rolling around when Luke told her to keep her day job. Maybe she'd make enough money for herself that she wouldn't feel like she was walking in GeeGee's deadly shadow just because they'd both killed a man that wanted to hurt them.

She thought of the syringe magically appearing in her hand. It was all the way across the room. She could never have reached it herself.

Gritting her teeth, she sighed despite the pain and opened the diary back up. She had reading to do. GeeGee wanted her to read it all, and she'd never gone wrong with following GeeGee's advice.

Out on the back patio, the wind chimes tinkled serenely.

As far as Delia could tell, there was no hint of a breeze.

ABOUT THE AUTHOR

Charlie Rhoads has decided to write thrillers to justify her obsession with true crime. She enjoys creepy houses, the flutter of her raised pulse in her throat, and both reading and writing things that make people afraid to turn out the light. Find her on Facebook.

Printed in Great Britain
by Amazon